Who hated the movie so much that they would commit arson?

"Fire!" Abby screamed. Where were those security guards?

She spotted a downed limb from a mesquite tree and used it to beat the flames, making some progress.... After what seemed hours,...other voices rang out, and Abby looked up to see uniformed men carrying blankets and racing toward her....

"Got another blanket?" she shouted at one of the men.

"Back there," he yelled.

...Abby snatched a blanket and saw that it was a skirt. They were using costumes from the movie to fight the fire....

"Over there," a policeman called, and Abby moved to the far edge of the field where the fire was rapidly spreading. She pounded the fiery ground until her arms felt like dead weights.

A siren alerted her to the fire engine zooming down the highway. Her mistake was watching it maneuver onto the field. When she looked back down, she saw a long tongue of fire had encircled her.

"Help!" she screamed.

"Abby!" she heard Milton shout.

She wrapped the blackened skirt around her bare legs to protect them...so she could make a dash through the fire.

"Abby!" another voice yelled.

"Rob!"

The tall man beat at the flames like a madman, cutting a narrow path through the fire. Abby rushed toward him, tripped on the skirt, and fell into his arms.

Veda Boyd Jones writes romances "that confirm my own values." Jones lives with her husband, an architect, and three sons in the Ozarks of Missouri.

Books by Veda Boyd Jones

HEARTSONG PRESENTS

HP21—Gentle Persuasion

Under
a Texas Sky

Veda Boyd Jones

Heartsong Presents

For Jimmie, with love

Thanks to Pam, Gordon, and Emily Trice for their hospitality in Abilene. And thanks to Landon, Morgan, and Marshall for exploring Fort Phantom Hill with me.

Scripture quoted by permission. Quotations designated (NIV) are from the THE HOLY BIBLE: NEW INTERNATIONAL VERSION. Copyright 1973, 1978, 1984 by The International Bible Society.

ISBN 1-55748-406-6

UNDER A TEXAS SKY

PRINTED IN THE U.S.A.

one

A tall, handsome man stepped out of an old stone building and squinted at the sun. He wore a cowboy hat, and a gun belt hung over his shoulder.

"I'm going into Abilene to talk to the sheriff. I'll be back before the stage pulls in," he said to someone inside the stone building. He pushed his Stetson up and gazed at the sky again, slowly pivoting his head a quarter turn as if he were looking for storm clouds, although the Texas sky was perfectly clear.

As he strapped on his gun, he called over his shoulder, "Take care, Callie," then he walked to his horse and climbed on.

"Cut!" the director called. "That's a print. Were all three cameras rolling?"

"We got it," said a cameraman, who sat at least ten feet off the ground in a bucket lift.

"Good job, Chase. Take fifteen, then we'll get some range shots."

Chase Cooper tipped his hat, acknowledging the compliment.

"That's it?" Abby said to her friend Barb, as the large crowd behind the film crew started buzzing. Barb had insisted they drive out to Fort Phantom Hill by eight, not allowing Abby the luxury of a Saturday morning sleep-in.

"Yeah, what were you expecting?"

"I don't know. Maybe a whole scene. Not just one person looking at the sky."

"That's how they do things in movies. This is my third day watching and it still fascinates me. Oh, look, here he comes." Barb stood spellbound as Chase Cooper passed within five yards of them.

"Are you going to spend your entire summer vacation out here in the heat swooning over movie stars?" Abby asked.

"Not the entire summer. They'll be through shooting here within a month. They work fast, even if it is in little pieces. Oh, there are my neighbors," Barb said and waved. "Half of Abilene is out here."

"I know," Abby agreed. She had already run into her mother and sister. "Let's get a drink," Abby suggested, and the two women walked toward the road where an enterprising teenager was selling cold drinks. The back of his pickup held not a cooler, but a horse trough full of ice and cans of pop.

They paid for their drinks and found some shade under a short mesquite tree close to one of the movie trailers.

"What's the plot of this movie?" Abby asked.

"Don't you read the newspaper?" her friend countered.

"Yes, I read the paper and I know about the movie, just not the plot. Unlike you with the schoolteacher tan, I have to be at work by eight o'clock so I don't get to leisurely read the paper and drink coffee on the porch."

"Okay, okay. You know, that's the third time today you've mentioned my schoolteacher tan. Are you hinting at something?"

Abby looked at her dark friend whose honey brown hair

sparkled with streaks of sunlight. Even if Abby had the summers off from her job at the Texas Tourist Bureau, with her fair complexion so common to redheads, she would never have the golden look of her friend.

She had snapped at Barb a couple of times and was ashamed of herself. She'd been working overtime, covering for her co-workers as they took vacation time. She was tired of work and tired of routine, but that was no reason to take it out on Barb. They had been best friends since they had met at their church singles group. Abby would do nothing to jeopardize their closeness.

"No," she said apologetically and shook her head. "I'm not hinting at anything. I'm just tired. Next week can't be over too soon. Then I'm on vacation, and for two weeks I'll thoroughly read the paper. I guarantee it. I don't know why my best friend is a teacher, but I sometimes feel a bit envious of your summers off, that's all. Now, what's the plot of this movie?"

"The good guy—and that's Chase Cooper if you hadn't noticed—"

"I'd noticed," Abby inserted.

"Well, he's going to save the heroine from the ghost of Fort Phantom Hill. She's a spunky gal who's running the stagecoach station by herself and someone's trying to scare her away. The newspaper article didn't tell who the ghost is, so I'm going to watch all the filming until I find out."

"Fort Phantom Hill was only used as a way station for a couple years. And that was before Abilene was a town," Abby scoffed. "If the hero is at the stagecoach station, he can't ride ten miles into a town that didn't exist then. The writer should have done some research."

"Is that true?" a deep masculine voice said from the side of the trailer.

Abby turned to stare into the bluest eyes she had ever seen on a man. No wonder Chase Cooper was becoming a big box office draw.

"Yes," she said in a squeaky voice she didn't recognize as her own. She'd never met a movie star before, and she had to force herself to continue in a more normal voice. "Abilene didn't exist when the Butterfield Stage Line had a way station here." She gestured to the ruins of the old fort. Only a few stone buildings and some stark chimneys remained of the fort that had been mysteriously burned.

"You know a lot about the history of this place?" he asked.

"I'm an Abilene native. I grew up playing among these ruins," Abby said. "My folks own a ranch not far from here." She felt as if she were babbling. Chase Cooper didn't care where she grew up.

"Would you come talk to our director?" he asked. "He prides himself on western films that are as historically correct as possible."

"Well, I. . ."

"Of course, she would," Barb said. "By the way, I'm Barb McDermid and this is my friend, Abby Kane." She held out her hand and Chase Cooper shook it briefly.

He didn't introduce himself, but motioned for them to accompany him. "This way."

He ushered the two women to a trailer a few yards away and opened the door for them to enter before him. Abby and Barb exchanged nervous glances.

"Sid, we've got a little problem," he said to a short, balding man in his fifties. "Abilene didn't exist when the stage stopped here."

"Great! Just what I need is another problem. This place must be jinxed," Sid exclaimed. "Who told you that?"

Chase looked at Abby as if waiting for her to explain.

"I did," she spoke up. "The guard house was only used as a way station for a couple of years in the late 1850s. Abilene didn't become a town until twenty years later."

"How do you know?" Sid asked.

"She's a native," Chase replied.

"She also runs the Texas Tourist Bureau in Abilene," Barb chimed in. "You couldn't have a better source on local history than Abby. She knows anything that happened in Texas, and when and where and how to get there. She's written brochures about them."

"Humm," Sid said. "Half the film takes place in Abilene."

"Perhaps you could just leave out the part about the stagecoach stopping at Fort Phantom Hill," Abby suggested.

"Humm," Sid said again. "My work is art. It's a tribute to a time when men were men and pitted their wits against the elements. I film authentic westerns. I can't let this just slip by. What would the critics say?"

Abby glanced at Barb, who was staring at Chase.

"We'll have to work it out. Where's Rob?" Sid asked a woman with a clipboard. "Get Rob."

He seemed to have dismissed her, so Abby turned to leave.

"Wait," Sid said. "Would you be willing to read the script and point out any other historical inaccuracies? Be sort of a historical consultant?"

"Maybe we're just making a mountain out of a mole-hill," Abby said. "Actually, most of the viewers won't know the difference. You could just keep it like it is."

"No," Sid said. "Could we buy just a little of your time—if you do know all you say about the history of the area?"

Feeling insulted, Abby drew herself up to her full height, all sixty-three inches of it.

"I'm a Texan. I have lived all my life in this area. My parents own the ranch a mile east of here, and I was raised on tales of Fort Phantom Hill. As a matter of fact, my great-grandfather was one of the first settlers in Abilene. I also have access to all sorts of local histories we use to prepare pamphlets at the bureau."

"Good," Sid said. "Sit," he ordered and took a chair at the work table. Abby sat down beside him. "Where's Rob?" he said impatiently to no one in particular.

As if on cue, the trailer door swung open and in strode a good-looking man in his early thirties wearing a Chicago Cubs baseball cap followed by the woman with the clipboard. He glanced at Abby, Chase, and Barb, then turned his attention to the director.

"Sid?"

"We've got a problem. The script doesn't seem to match the history books. I want you to fix it. This woman knows Texas history. She'll help you." He turned to Abby. "What's your name?"

"Abby Kane."

"Rob Vincent," the man in the cap introduced himself and smiled at her.

"Get her a script, Rob, and then talk it through. Work all night if you have to. I want a report first thing tomorrow morning."

"Sure, Sid." Rob faced Abby. "Looks like we'll be working together. If you'll come with me, please."

Abby followed him out of the trailer and into the heat of the June morning. Barb reluctantly trailed after them and Abby introduced her to Rob. Chase Cooper stayed in the air-conditioned trailer with the director.

"Wait," Abby said as Rob Vincent led them toward another trailer. "I'm not sure exactly what's going on here. I simply made the remark that Abilene didn't exist when Fort Phantom Hill was used as a way station. The next thing I know, I'm talking to Chase Cooper and the director. And now I'm a consultant?"

Rob grinned. "That's the movie business for you, Abby. It moves fast. Everything has to be done by yesterday." He opened the door of the trailer in front of them. "I'll be right back."

"What have you gotten me into?" Abby said to her friend.

"Me?" Barb answered. "You're the one who was spouting the history. Besides, I think it's exciting. Just think, we've met Chase Cooper."

"Wow," Abby said, although she admitted to herself that she had been a bit flustered when she had talked to the actor. "I didn't even ask that Sid person how much he's going to pay me for some of my valuable time."

"That Sid person! That's Sid Kellough, the director. He won an Oscar two years ago. Who cares what he pays? Imagine getting to read the script of *The Ghost of Fort*

Phantom Hill."

"This sounds too much like helping tourists at the bureau and not at all like how I planned on spending my weekend."

"What would you be doing? Laundry? Cleaning your house?"

"I have a date with Milton tonight."

"That's as thrilling as doing laundry. Get rid of that guy. This is a chance of a lifetime." Barb held out her hands in a dramatic gesture.

"A chance of a lifetime," Abby echoed. "I suppose it is." She looked around the once deserted fort, now full of activity, and felt a tingle of excitement shake off the tiredness she'd felt before.

"Hi, Mr. Turner," she called to the old man who lived on the land next to her parents' ranch. "Enjoying the show?"

Never one for words, Mr. Turner grunted in reply as he scuttled into the crowd of spectators and crew.

The door to the trailer opened and Rob descended the three steps to the ground.

"Let's go over to a quiet spot," he said.

"I'm going to watch the next scene," Barb said. "Catch you later."

Rob led Abby across the main road, heading away from the crowd, and followed an old trail toward a pond. Halfway around the pond, he stopped under the shade of a large tree and motioned for Abby to sit on the ground.

"This is my tree," Abby said.

"You planted this tree?" Rob said, looking up at the huge branches. "It appears to be much older than you."

"No. I grew up about a mile from here. This is where I always came when I wanted to be alone to sort out problems—my place to think."

It had always been a special place to her—a place where she could talk to God and commune with nature. A place where peace settled upon her and troubles seemed small. She called it her prayer tree, but she didn't take time to wonder why she hadn't mentioned that to Rob.

"I discovered it myself a couple days ago," he said and smiled at her. "It's peaceful here." He patted the trunk of the large tree. "I'll bet this is the prettiest tree around for a hundred miles. Makes the rest of these," he waved at the short mesquite trees, "look like supporting actors. I thought everything was big in Texas."

"Except mesquite trees," Abby said. "They're purposely small so we can reach the mistletoe at Christmastime." She pointed to a clump of the parasite.

"So that's what that is. I've never seen it growing."

"Stick around and you'll see lots of things you've never seen. This is Texas. Everything is bigger and better here."

"Spoken like a true Texan," he said and laughed. He handed Abby the script he had carried. She flipped it open to the first page.

"You wrote this?" she asked, wondering how she could work with a man who was responsible for rewriting history.

"No. I mean, yes. I wrote the screenplay. It's based on a book by E. L. Minton. He's the one who didn't do his homework, although I should have thought to check the story for chronological problems. Sid's such a stickler for history."

Rob took off his ball cap, exposing a mop of curly blond hair, and wiped the back of his hand across his brow. "It sure is hot for June."

"It'll get hotter," Abby said.

He grinned and Abby caught herself staring at him, now that the cap was gone and she could get a good look. Laugh lines crinkled around intelligent eyes that rivaled those of Chase Cooper, although they were a lighter shade of blue. His nose appeared a bit crooked, as if it had been broken once, and his wide grin revealed even white teeth. His tan told her he spent a good bit of time in the sun, even if he was a writer. Maybe he wrote out of doors. She imagined him on a California patio by a pool instead of under a shade tree by a Texas pond.

"Do you want me to read this here?" Abby asked as a gust of wind riffled the pages of the script.

"Can you think of a better place?"

"We could go into town and work in the library. While I read this, you could read a couple of local histories, then we could talk."

"An excellent idea," Rob said and stood up. He reached down and gave Abby a hand. When he pulled her up she stood inches from him and that close, she had to tilt her head back to see his face. She hadn't realized he was so tall.

"I need to find Barb," Abby said as they followed the trail back to the fort. "Oh, do you have a car? I rode out here with my friend," Abby explained.

"I can get one easily enough. The company's rented quite a few for our use. I'll get a key. Meet me by the soda pop truck?"

Abby nodded and walked through the crowd of some

two hundred people until she located Barb. She explained about the library.

"Want to go with us?" Abby asked.

"I think I'll stick around and watch the action. They'll be filming a lot today. I heard a crew member say they were on a pretty tight schedule. A lot of Chase's solo shots will be done before Penny Lynn gets here on Monday. Imagine, Penny Lynn here in Abilene," Barb said.

"Pretty exciting stuff," Abby said, beginning to fall under the spell herself.

"This is an event, Abby. There may never be another movie filmed in Abilene. I don't want to miss any of it."

"All right. If you're sure you don't want to go with us."

"If you want me to, I will," Barb said. "Are you afraid of going off with a guy you just met?"

"Not at all." Abby's eyes widened. "Isn't that funny? I don't even think of him as a stranger."

"Because he looks like a long, tall Texan?" Barb said and laughed.

Abby thought for a moment. "That's probably it," she said, but admitted to herself that it was because he had found her favorite place in the world and thought it was special, too.

two

"You'll have to direct me," Rob said as they neared the highway that bypassed the city. "Until we landed here, I had no idea that Abilene was so big. Actually, I thought it was in Kansas."

Abby laughed and in her official tourist bureau voice said, "Abilene has almost a hundred thousand residents. It was named after Abilene, Kansas, because that was the end of the cattle drive and this was the beginning." She pointed to the right. "Take the next exit."

Within ten minutes they arrived at the city library. Abby introduced Rob to Marilee, the librarian in the reference department, and explained what they needed.

"We close at six today. But since you must rewrite that by tomorrow, I'll let you take whatever you need with you," the librarian said. Marilee spoke to Abby, but her eyes rested appreciatively on Rob.

She's looking at him like Barb looks at Chase Cooper, Abby thought. There was a magic about show people. Everyone was in awe of them, including herself. They seemed unreal, as if their everyday lives had nothing in common with the everyday lives of the people in Abilene. That old saying that every man puts his pants on one leg at a time didn't seem to ring true with movie people. Maybe because they lived in a make-believe world.

Oh, well. There was no use analyzing it to death. Her

contact with the movie industry would be short-lived. By this time tomorrow, she and Rob would have met with Sid, given him what they had come up with, and that would be that. She would return to her normal world and everyday demands like laundry and tourists.

"Where would you like to sit?" Rob asked, bringing Abby's wayward thoughts back to the business at hand.

"How about here? We'll be close to the reference area."

Rob set his books on the table and took the chair across from Abby.

"I guess you need to read the script all the way through, making notes of the areas that defy history," he suggested.

Abby nodded and pushed back her chair. "I'll get some paper," she told him.

She spied a friend across the library and asked to borrow some notebook paper. Of course she had to explain what she was doing in the library with such a handsome fellow and then had to introduce Steffie to Rob before she could secure the needed paper.

"You're creating quite a stir here," Abby told Rob as she again took her seat at the table.

"I'm used to it," Rob said.

Abby's eyebrows shot up in surprise at his arrogance.

"Oh, it's not me," he quickly assured her. "It's the movie business. Most people think it's glamorous."

"And it's not?"

"Living in a motel for weeks at a time is not glamorous, but you can't tell someone that. They wouldn't believe you. And besides, it'd blow the image, and image is what movies are all about."

"But you just told me."

He grinned. "You seem the down-to-earth type who wouldn't harbor a secret dream of being an actress. I'm trusting you with important knowledge," he said and winked.

Abby nodded and looked away. She dug a pen out of her purse and straightened the few sheets of paper, hoping her movements would cover her inner feelings.

She was not pleased that he would call her a down-to-earth type. What did that mean anyway? Homely? No, wholesome. A boy she had dated years ago in high school had told her she was wholesome. She didn't like it then and she didn't like it now.

But was it true? Her big plans for the weekend were to do the domestic chores that she had neglected during the work week, have a date with Milton, teach her Sunday school class, and relax with a book. The same routine she'd had since coming back to Abilene.

And what about Milton? Was he as boring as Barb thought? Probably. Dull. Her life was dull. She needed some excitement, a change of pace. And wasn't it here, staring her in the face?

She felt a twinge of guilt. Milton Womack was a fine Christian man whom she admired. They had a lot in common. They attended the same church and they both felt the importance of family. But she had to admit there was no spark between them. Was Milton just a comfortable habit she'd fallen into? Compared to Rob, Milton paled in significance. Rob was a dynamic, in-charge personality.

Abby shrugged her shoulders, as if to dismiss her guilt, and opened the script. This was an opportunity of a lifetime—even if the actual experience would only be for twenty-four hours. She would get to know another side of life: Hollywood. She would grab life by the horns—the Texas longhorns—and go for it.

Abby read for the next couple of hours, making notes as she went. She took a break to call Milton and cancel their date, then read some more. Rob got up and down, getting new material to review. When she had finished the last page, Abby looked up to find Rob's gaze on her.

"Let's go eat. I'm famished," he said.

Abby glanced at her watch. It was past one.

"You should have stopped me," she said.

"I wanted you to finish so we could talk over lunch. In the movie industry, a business lunch is quite the in thing."

"Then let's go," Abby said. "I certainly want to do the in thing."

She gathered up the script and her notes, and Rob returned his book to the reference desk.

"Will you be back?" the librarian asked.

"Of course," he said. "You've been a big help to me."

The librarian almost purred.

Abby glanced at Rob as he took her elbow and guided her out of the library.

"Image," he said. "It's the image."

"Did you ever think it might be the man?" she asked.

He looked thoughtful. "Only on rare occasions. Mostly women want to know me so I can introduce them to the actors."

"That's terrible," Abby said.

"Yes, it is. But it's a who-you-know world, and a lot of women want to get to know Chase or Sid or whoever I'm working with at the time who has some power in the industry. That old shot-at-stardom dream comes into play and I'm left behind."

"You've known a special woman who was after that shot?" Abby guessed.

"Yes," he said as he opened the car door for her.

"Sorry," she offered.

"Hey," he said and shrugged. "It's life. I accept it and I go on. What about you? Anyone special who broke your heart once upon a time? Or is there anyone special now?"

Abby waited until he had climbed in on his side before she replied. "No, no one special," she said and knew she was speaking the truth. There really was no future with Milton. She just had not realized it before. And the other men she occasionally dated certainly fell into the friend category.

He backed out of the parking spot.

"Which way? What sounds good?"

They decided on pizza, and Abby directed him to her favorite place, a mom and pop outfit that specialized in Italian food.

"The food's as good as the decor," she told him as they were led to a high-backed, ornately carved wooden booth.

"What a great place," Rob said, looking around at the other booths before he sat down in their own private world, closed off from the rest of the restaurant. "They've decorated it to look like turn of the century style."

"No. It's original turn of the century. This restaurant has changed hands a few times since it was started almost a hundred years ago, but the booths have always remained. It's been Cidadino's for the last forty years."

They ordered a pizza with everything on it and a couple soft drinks. Abby opened the script and pulled out her notes.

"Well, what do you think?" Rob asked.

"I thought there would be more conversation than there is. I know everything is dialogue, but the blocking directions take up a lot of the script. Some scenes have only music and, of course, the action." She dug in her purse and found a pen.

"The days when the hero says, 'I'm going to get on my horse' and then does it, are over," Rob explained. "Audiences are more sophisticated now and don't need to be spoon-fed everything. How many problems did you find?"

"Really only the one, the stagecoach way station being at Fort Phantom Hill, but it crops up over and over and is certainly the reason Callie is living out there by herself."

He sighed. "Okay. We want to keep Abilene in the script. We're already scheduled to shoot at Buffalo Gap."

Abby nodded her understanding that the local replica of a western town would be a perfect movie set. Tourists already stopped there, but this publicity would give Buffalo Gap added appeal.

"We've got to come up with another reason for her to be out at the fort. It doesn't have to be truthful, but it has to be believable," Rob said.

"I thought Sid was a stickler for the truth." Abby moved the script to the side so the waitress could set down the drinks.

"He is, but we're dealing with a piece of fiction. A glaring error like chronology that's off isn't believable. But we can make up a good reason for Callie to be out at

Fort Phantom Hill."

"Does she have to be alone?"

"She does if we bring our hero Trice in to help her find the supposed ghost who's haunting the place. Otherwise those two characters wouldn't meet and we wouldn't have a story. Now let's be creative."

They talked and talked, rejecting idea after idea. Some because they weren't believable. Some because they wouldn't fit historically. As soon as Abby jotted down an idea, she crossed it out.

The pizza came and disappeared two pieces at a time. Rob ordered a second round of pop.

"Did you know that the fort is privately owned property and always has been?" Abby asked. "Maybe Callie could have inherited it. She's staying there because she has no money and nowhere else to go."

"Why would she be alone?"

"Maybe her family was killed by Indians. No," Abby quickly discarded that idea. "The Comanches in the area weren't exactly friendly, but they never assaulted the fort."

"Shall we go back to the library? Maybe we'll find something there," Rob suggested. He picked up the check and ushered Abby to the front of the restaurant.

"A receipt, please," he said to the cashier. "Expenses," he told Abby.

"Abby, Abby, it's good to see you again," Mama Cidadino called from the doorway to the kitchen. "Who's your young man?"

Abby introduced Rob and noticed the immediate change in the older woman when she learned that Rob was involved with the movie.

"My Nicki went out to see them film. She should be in movies herself, that one. Very easy on the eyes. Like Abby here."

"Yes," Rob said. "Abby's pretty enough to be in pictures, but I'm glad she doesn't have that goal." He placed a hand on her shoulder.

"Abby's a good one. Not many like her. Smart and pretty. Better not let her get away," Mama advised.

If she had been the kind to blush, Abby knew she would be beet red.

"I'll keep that advice in mind," Rob said, and keeping his hand on her shoulder, steered Abby outside. He opened the car door for her.

"I've known Mama Cidadino all my life. She's loud, sometimes obnoxious, and she always manages to embarrass me," Abby complained when he joined her in the car. "I don't know why I keep coming back here."

"Because you like her and her food," Rob said simply.

"You're right," Abby answered and quickly changed the subject back to the problem with the movie script. "There once was a town that grew up around the fort, but when the railroad came through here, the town disappeared. The people probably moved to Abilene. I don't know much about it, but maybe Callie could stay there for some reason."

"Sounds like a possibility. Let's check out that town and see if there's anything we could use."

Back at the library, the two poured over several old volumes, looking for a mention of the town. Abby left Rob with a thick diary and asked the librarian for the census reports for the late eighteen hundreds.

She sat isolated at a microfilm reader-printer reading year after year of entries. Finally, Abby found what she was looking for. She made a print and went back to the table to tell Rob her news.

The table was empty. There was no Rob, even her notes and the script were missing.

Abby glanced at her watch. Ten after six. She hadn't realized it was so late. The library should have closed ten minutes ago, but the lights were still on.

She looked around nervously. Not a soul in sight. Was she locked in the library? Would Rob have left her here alone?

A woman's laugh caused Abby to twirl and follow the sound to the workroom behind the reference counter. Rob sat behind a large desk in a swivel chair while the reference librarian sat on the desk facing him. Two other women employees sat on the hard chairs against the wall, all hanging onto every word Rob uttered.

"Of course that was the first time it happened, but not the last," Rob was saying. "You never know what animals will do on the set. All the lights and the people make them nervous."

He looked up and caught Abby watching from the doorway.

"Ready, Abby? I have some books that Marilee said we could take with us."

"Good," Abby said.

"Do you have to go?" Marilee asked. "If you want to stay and read microfilm, Abby, I'll wait around to lock up."

I'll just bet you would, Abby thought, and then was

shocked by her own emotions. She felt as if these women were trespassing on her territory when she had only known Rob a total of eight hours. It must be the movie business. Rob had told her it moved fast, and she was caught right up in the action.

"No, I'm finished with the census reports. But thanks for the offer. Rob and I can finish this at my house." She didn't know why she had said that.

"Ladies, it's been a pleasure," Rob said as he pushed the chair back and stood up. He picked up three books. "Thanks for these, Marilee. Do I need to sign for them?"

"Yes. This autograph might be worth big bucks someday," she said and laughed. She wrote down the titles and Rob signed his name.

"Thanks again," he said as he walked to the doorway.

He placed his hand on Abby's shoulder, just as he had in the restaurant. *It must be a Hollywood thing*, she thought, hating to admit that she liked it. As Rob guided her to the front door, Abby glanced back to see the librarians staring enviously after them.

"So, we're headed to your house," Rob said.

"Unless you can think of a better place."

"No," he said. "I'm not fond of my hotel room. We can work for a while and then get something for dinner."

"It's not far," she said and gave him directions.

As he drove, Abby noticed how totally in command he was of the car. He seemed to be in command of his life, too. She sensed that little could rattle him. *The strong, silent type*, she thought, *just like in the movies*. Except he wasn't really silent. He had talked openly with her and certainly had charmed the librarians in a short while.

"Turn left. It's the corner house."

Rob pulled smoothly into the driveway of the two-story house.

"You live here alone?"

"Yes. I know it's a bit big, but it was my grandparents' home at one time. I had some great childhood memories of the place, so when it came on the market two years ago, I jumped at the chance to buy it. Of course, I only own the front porch and the bank owns the rest," she said and laughed. "The last owners had different tastes than mine, so I've been putting my own touches on it little by little."

She unlocked the front door and led the way into a large entry hall. She motioned to French doors on the left. "Living room in there. Bedroom down that hall." She pointed to the right. "And to the back is the kitchen."

"This staircase is fantastic," Rob said, rubbing his hand along the smooth stained wood.

"Thanks. The previous owners painted it. It took me forever to strip and refinish it. I've closed off the upstairs. Too expensive to cool, although I have redecorated one bedroom up there. The next room I tackle is a study." Actually it was going to be a special writing room for her secret ambition. A very private place. "I'm going to start—"

The phone rang, interrupting her.

"I'll bet that's Barb," she said and walked into the kitchen to answer the wall phone. "She's so impressed with the movie and with Chase Cooper."

Rob followed Abby into the kitchen.

"Hello. I knew it was you," she said and winked at Rob. *He's got me winking*, Abby thought. How effortlessly he had influenced her.

As Abby explained about her day at the library, Rob walked around the large kitchen and plopped the books and script on the kitchen table that set at one end.

"Ask her if she'd like to have dinner with Chase," Rob said.

"Just a minute, Barb. What did you say?"

"I was thinking it would be great to fix some Chinese food for supper." He motioned toward the wok that set on the long counter. "It's Chase's favorite. He'd come in a minute."

"Barb, listen carefully. Would you like to come over for Chinese? Chase Cooper may come."

Abby held the phone away from her ear and could still hear Barb's shriek.

"Wait a minute. Would you stop by the store and pick up bean sprouts, water chestnuts—"

"I'll go," Rob interrupted. "Tell her to get here about seven and that you'll call her back if Chase can't come over."

Abby relayed the message and rang off.

"You really think Chase will come over here for dinner?"

For an answer, Rob picked up the receiver and dialed the hotel. "Room 902, please."

"Would you like something to drink?" Abby asked while he was waiting to be connected to Chase's room. "Iced tea?"

"Sounds good," he said, then turned his attention to the phone.

"Chase, would you like homemade Chinese?" He grinned

at the answer which Abby couldn't hear. "We've got an apron with your name on it. Tell you what, I'll pick you up in a few minutes and we can shop for your specialties." There was a pause then, "Yes, at Abby's. I'll tell you all about it later."

He hung up the phone and turned to Abby. "He'd be delighted. Let's make a list of supplies. Abby, you don't mind, do you? This kitchen looks so inviting after a few days of restaurant meals. It's so homey."

"I don't mind. But what about the script?"

"We'll let Chase and Barb chop all the vegetables while we work. Hey, we'll let them cook it, too. But there's one thing you should tell Barb. Chase has a girlfriend already. Actually a fiancée. She's a fine woman, and he's true blue. I don't want Barb to get the wrong idea. I just thought it would be nice for her to get to know him better. He's a nice guy, a good friend of mine, and he could use a few hours of relaxation."

"I'll tell her," Abby said.

"Good. I'll go get Chase and some groceries. Do you have rice?"

"Yes."

"Would you go ahead and make it so it can cool? We'll have fried rice."

"Sure," she replied and looked through the pantry.

Rob wrote out a shopping list. "Be back in half an hour," he called as he left.

Abby measured the rice and water into a pan, then called Barb to give her Rob's message.

"Hey, I'm not so star struck that I'd imagine a romance," Barb said. "I'm just thrilled to get to talk to him. And over dinner. Wow! This movie making is the most exciting thing that's ever happened to me."

"And to me," Abby said and meant it.

three

Barb arrived only minutes before Rob returned with a sack of groceries and Chase Cooper.

"Chase has to be back at work at nine, so we'll let them get right to cooking," Rob said.

Barb nervously turned to the actor. "You have to work tonight?"

"There's a full moon. We'll be getting some shots of me against the sky, the horse against the sky, the buckboard against the sky. We've got another outfit filming the sky at Buffalo Gap. I've got to go down there part of the night," Chase explained.

Abby placed chopping boards on the counters and got out her sharpest knifes.

"Barb, if you can't find something, ask. Do you like to cook, Chase?"

"Only Chinese. But don't let it get around. Not good for the image," he said and laughed.

Abby nodded. The Hollywood image again.

"Let's get to work, Abby," Rob said.

He followed her into the living room where Abby had arranged their work area. While he had been gone, she had moved her large Bible and Sunday school quarterly from the coffee table to an out-of-the-way bookshelf. Now the script, books, and Abby's notes lay by two glasses of iced tea on the square coffee table that separated a couch from two mismatched upholstered chairs.

Abby sat on the couch and reached for the script. Rob sat beside her.

"The author never mentions how Fort Phantom Hill got its name."

"I wondered about that," Rob said.

"From a distance in this flat area, Phantom Hill looks like a hill, but you never have the sense of climbing it or having ever reached the top. It's like a phantom that keeps retreating before you."

"That isn't an exciting explanation. Maybe that's why the author left it out," he suggested.

"There are lots of legends about it. The army officer's wife who set the fort on fire haunts the place. Or an Indian brave looking for his squaw is there—especially during a full moon. Then there's a band of soldiers who tried to desert but were caught. The story goes that they keep coming back as specters."

"That's more like it. We could add some of those stories and give the script more suspense."

"Can we change it like that?"

"Oh sure. Haven't you read a book then seen the movie and said the book was different?"

"Yes, I have." Abby nodded thoughtfully.

"Poetic license or something like that. Now, let's solve the problem of Callie being at the fort in the first place."

They talked and wrote and discussed some more. They paced and sat and ended up sitting on the floor, bent over the coffee table.

At the end of an hour Chase called them to dinner. Rob escorted Abby into the kitchen.

"Three entrees and fried rice," Abby exclaimed. "You two have been busy."

"Chinese is my specialty, my only specialty," Chase said. "Barb's a good chef's assistant."

They sat down and Barb looked expectantly at Abby, who lowered her eyes briefly as she secretly asked a blessing.

"What's this dish, Chase?" she asked brightly as she spooned some vegetables onto her plate.

The meal was enjoyed with pleasant camaraderie. It was almost as if the foursome had been friends for some time instead of two movie people having dinner with strangers. Abby noticed that Barb was no longer nervous around Chase, but kidded him with the same light banter she used around her own brother.

"Have you worked out the problems?" Chase asked.

"Yes, but now we have to clean up the script," Rob answered. "We're going to add a couple local legends to give more suspense. Abby's a good writer and a great researcher.

"We've got Callie living out there because her family lived at the fort but was wiped out by small pox. That wasn't uncommon. She stays out there because she promised her dad that she'd keep the farm that he's worked so hard for. He had hopes that the railroad would come through his land, but it's routed through Abilene, so the town around Callie dies.

"Because of the small pox germs, she burns their cabin and moves onto the fort, into the stone building that had been used as a way station in the 1850s. She has one neighbor a mile away and another neighbor two miles the other direction. She's not as isolated as she was in the first script, but it'll still work and let Abilene stay in the picture."

"Will you have it finished by tomorrow?" Chase asked.

"Should." Rob glanced at his watch. "Could be a late night. It's already eight-thirty."

"Hey, I've got to get to makeup. Will you drive me out, Rob?"

"You can take the car if Abby will give me a lift. Abby?"

"Sure," Abby quickly agreed.

"So, Chase," Barb said, as he pushed his chair back and prepared to leave. "Are you sticking me with the dishes?"

"You wouldn't expect a great chef to wash dishes?" he asked and laughed. "Abby, this has been great. Relaxing. I feel like a new person, actually in a home and in good company."

"Whenever you feel like cooking, please think of my kitchen first," she offered. She followed him into the entry, where he stopped automatically in front of the mirror and preened before leaving. "Come again, Chase," she called after him.

With Chase gone, Abby helped Barb clean up the kitchen while Rob worked alone outlining what changes needed to be made by morning.

"You and Chase seemed to get along great," Abby said.

"He's not such a big screen star after all," Barb informed her. "This is his fourth movie. The second one was such a hit that it made his name."

She turned to the sink but continued with Chase's biography. "The third one wasn't great, but he thinks this one will go. The resurgence of westerns could mean a new genre for him. He's been doing light comedies. He sees this movie as a more serious venture."

"He seems like a nice guy—maybe a little vain. I'm not as comfortable around him as you are, but then I didn't cook Chinese with Chase Cooper," Abby said and laughed as she loaded plates into the dishwasher.

"Ah, he's okay. He's an actor so you expect him to be vain. It takes a lot of arrogance to strut out in front of cameras and a ton of people and act like someone else. This is definitely going to be an exciting summer." Barb lowered her voice. "Rob seems like a real sweetie."

Abby glanced toward the doorway to make sure he wasn't within listening range. "Real sweetie doesn't quite do it. He's an intelligent, caring, sensitive man. And he certainly does charm the ladies. You ought to have seen the librarians swarm over him."

Barb chuckled. "Are you jealous, Abby?"

"Jealous of what? I just met him this morning."

"I know, but he kept watching you through dinner. I just thought there might be an interesting romance in the offing."

"Well, think again. He's a jet-setter and I'm a wholesome homebody. He's California and I'm Texas. And I'd better go see if I can help him with that script."

"Are you leaving me with these dishes, too?" Barb asked.

"We only lack washing the wok. The price you pay for an exciting summer," Abby said and went in to help Rob.

"How's it going?" she asked.

"We need to get back to my computer," Rob replied. "These lines need to be changed for tonight's shoot. It's not much, but mention of the stage has to be deleted."

"So where do we need to go? Your hotel or back to Fort Phantom Hill?"

"Fort Phantom Hill. I use a lap-top computer, and I should have brought it with me."

"Do you mind if Barb comes with us?"

"No, that's fine. As long as she doesn't keep us from working."

"You won't even know I'm there," Barb said from the doorway.

Rob grinned. "Now, why do I doubt that?" he teased.

The trio climbed into Abby's Chevy, Rob in the front beside her and Barb in the back seat.

When they arrived at Phantom Hill, it was not quite dark and the area around the fort was as crowded as it had been that morning.

"Where do all these people come from?" Barb asked.

"The first night shoot usually brings out the werewolves," Rob said. "After we've been here a week, the newness will wear off and you'll be hard pressed to find anyone from Abilene out here."

"Hi, Rob."

The group turned to see Marilee walking toward them.

"Did you finish the script? Were the books useful?" she said to Rob, ignoring the women.

"Not done yet, but the books were immensely helpful," Rob said. "Abby and I were just going back to work. Catch us later, Barb. See you, Marilee."

In one hand he held their script and notes. He let the other hand fall on Abby's shoulder, just as he had in the library, and led her toward a trailer.

"Are you using me for some sort of defense?" Abby accused him.

He grinned a lopsided grin. "I think she wants to be in movies," he said in an off-handed explanation.

"And therefore, she's after you to introduce her to someone with clout," Abby finished for him.

"Something like that. Here we are," he said and opened the door of the trailer where he had gotten the script earlier.

Abby climbed inside and looked around. This was a workroom, not unlike the trailer she had been in with the director. A conference table dominated the small area, with chairs around it for six.

Rob moved to the counter along one wall and picked up his computer. He assembled it on the table.

"Have a seat," he said and handed her a yellow see-through marker and the script. "Start on this page and mark every scene you find that has 'night shot' on it. I want to make sure we get every mention of that stage out of tonight's scenes."

Abby worked her way quickly through the script while Rob entered changes. When he had finished at the keyboard, he printed several pages.

"I'll take this over to Sid and tell him about the new scenes we're going to add." He tore the pages from the printer, separated them, and made copies on the copy machine.

"Look over this part and see if one of the legends will fit in," he said, handing Abby some pages. "I'll get a shooting schedule so we can stay ahead of the cameras. That'll buy us a little time. Be right back," he called over his shoulder.

Left alone, Abby concentrated on the script. It was difficult working like this. When she had written brochures for the bureau, she had started at the beginning and told a story, not jumped right in the middle.

She looked up when the door opened and recognized the woman with the clipboard from the morning's discussion with Sid. She was thirty-something with blond hair pulled back from her face and fastened with a big red bow.

"How's it going with Rob?" the woman asked.

"Fine. He's talking with Sid."

"I know. I'm Emily Wilson," she said. "Sid's right arm, although I do have a fancy title that I can't remember."

Abby laughed and introduced herself. "You do anything and everything he tells you to do?"

"And try to foresee some of the problems." She stepped over to the copy machine.

"Have you run into many?"

"Some. A practical joker struck this afternoon. Our portable toilets were treated with some sort of chemical that made them smell horrible. Sulphur of some sort."

"Did you catch whoever did it?"

"Not a clue. There were too many spectators around to notice any one person."

Emily ran some copies and tacked one sheet on the bulletin board above the counter.

"Tomorrow's shooting schedule. Everyone gets a schedule, but we post one just the same. They lose them, misplace them. Sometimes they act like school kids on a holiday."

"Is it like that for you, Emily? A holiday every time you go on location?"

"Sometimes yes, sometimes no. It's according to how the shooting goes. The location doesn't matter because we're usually too busy to notice. Today we got a break from five to nine since we'll be shooting a lot tonight. Still, I didn't get to see any of the countryside because of Sid's demands. Hi, Rob," she said as the door opened again.

"Hey, Emily, is that the schedule you have there?"

"Sure is. What'll you give me for it?" she teased.

For answer, Rob reached over and gave her a quick kiss on the cheek.

"That'll do it, honey," Emily said and laughed, handing him one of the sheets from her stack of copies.

"Sid likes the changes we're going to make, but he still wants to see the whole thing tomorrow," he told Abby.

"Okay. I think we could work better starting at the beginning anyway."

Emily and Rob both laughed as if what she had said was a big joke.

"We all felt that way at first," Emily explained. "I remember seeing the first movie I worked on. I was amazed at the story line. When we filmed it, I saw it in such disjointed parts, I couldn't see what event led to the next."

"Going straight through will help," Rob said. "But we still may pull an all-nighter."

"I'll get out of the way, so you can get at it," Emily said and opened the door. "It was nice meeting you, Abby. I'm sure I'll see you around."

Rob pulled out a chair and sat down beside Abby.

"All right. We'll go through and add new information where it's appropriate. Remember motivation has to be there for every scene we write."

"Motivation?"

"There has to be a reason for every movement by every character."

Rob pulled out their list of legends and the changes required to work in the small pox story and the desertion of the town that had grown up around the fort. While Abby jotted notes on the script, he made changes on the computer. After two hours, they had finished almost half the script.

"Break time," Rob announced. "Let's get a drink and some fresh air."

They stepped out of the trailer, which was only one in a complex of six trailers parked in two rows.

"You've been in Sid's office," Rob said, and pointed to the trailer where Abby had been that morning. "The big semi is like a control booth. Lots of monitors, lots of equipment. Makeup is here, wardrobe and dressing rooms in this one, generator here," he pointed again, "and here we are at the most important one. Since we're on a western location, we'll call it the chuck wagon. How about a drink?"

"Anything diet," Abby replied. "None of the crew sleeps out here?"

"We're close enough to town to stay at motels, and believe me they are more comfortable than the cramped quarters we sometimes endure. They also have dining rooms, swimming pools, all the amenities, although we don't usually have time for much of that."

He went into the chuck wagon and returned shortly carrying two soft drink cans.

"The crowd is over by the commissary storehouse,"

Abby said. "What part are they filming there?"

"Remember the scene where Callie hears something outside and Trice goes out to check the stock?" he asked and Abby nodded. "He doesn't catch anyone, but it's the first time he sees signs of digging. The full moon will give a sense of what he finds, but he'll go back out at first light to check it again and find the hole gone."

"Will you be filming at dawn tomorrow?"

"No. Sometime next week that part will be shot and they'll get as many of the early morning shots as they can at one time. We need rain for the scene where Trice captures the bad guy. So the first sign of a sprinkle we'll be out here, day or night."

"This is fascinating," Abby said. "I had no idea how a movie was made. I can understand Barb's interest. Oh, we ought to tell her it's going to be a late night."

"As soon as they finish this bit, we can walk over to the crowd and find her." No sooner had Rob uttered the words than the crowd began talking and breaking apart. "Now's a good time," he said. He placed his arm around Abby's shoulder as they walked toward the camera area.

"Do you see Marilee?" Abby asked.

"No. Oh," he said as he realized what she meant. "You're the perfect size for me to rest an arm here," he said. "And I like doing it," he said softly and looked into her eyes. "Do you mind?"

Abby didn't mind a bit. It felt right and it felt good. But she knew the gesture was a Hollywood mannerism, just like Rob pecking Emily's cheek in the work trailer. Or she hoped that kiss was simply the posturing that went with the industry. There didn't seem to be anything between Rob and Emily.

"It's all right," she said finally. "Barb!" she called as she saw her friend.

"I saw your folks out here," Barb said as soon as she joined them. "They've gone now, but I told them about your job. They were impressed."

"Speaking of jobs, we need to get back to work. It's going to be a long night. I could take you home, then come back," she said and looked at Rob for approval.

"Oh, no," Barb said. "They're not through here yet, then they're moving down to Buffalo Gap. I've been watching with Cathy and Mark, two other schoolteachers," she explained to Rob. "I'll catch a ride with them."

"Okay. Have fun," Abby said.

"We'll see you later, Barb," Rob said and again rested his arm on Abby's shoulder as they walked back to the trailer.

By one o'clock in the morning, they lacked only twenty pages, and most of those didn't need changing.

"I can finish, if you'd like to go on home," Rob offered.

"And how would you get back to the hotel?" Abby asked as she stretched her weary arms above her head and yawned.

"With you. I can take the computer with me."

"And then set it up again when you get to the hotel? That's too much trouble. Let's just get it done."

"Thanks. It's going a lot faster with both of us working."

"Rob, I'm not adding much. I'm merely a sounding board for you."

"Believe me, that helps. I don't sound so crazy when I'm talking out loud."

Within another half-hour, they had finished the script and Rob had printed out the final pages.

"We'll make copies tomorrow," he said. "Sid wants to see us at eight. Can you make it on a few hours sleep?"

"Sure. How long will the meeting take? I have an engagement at nine-thirty that I really can't break."

Why didn't she tell him she had a Sunday school class to teach and it was too late to find a substitute?

"We'll be finished by then. Let's get out of here."

Rob opened the door for Abby and then turned out the light and followed her into the night air. Only the full moon illuminated the eerie ruins, causing a shiver to run down Abby's spine.

"I didn't realize everyone was gone," she whispered.

"They're over at Buffalo Gap getting a few pictures of the full moon against that setting," Rob said quietly.

As they walked away from the trailers, Abby heard something and turned toward the spot where the bake house had stood. Only a lone chimney remained. A ghostly reminder of what once had been.

"Did you hear that?" she whispered.

"No," he said, his voice sounding loud in the still night.

They walked on toward Abby's car.

"There it is again. There's someone over there, Rob."

"Abby, you're letting your imagination run away with you—and I don't blame you. It's spooky out here."

Abby glanced back over her shoulder.

"Look!" she cried.

four

Abby stood frozen as she stared at a figure of a woman in a bonnet and a long skirt that dragged the ground.

"Hey, what are you doing there?" Rob called. He strode toward the woman. "Do you need some help?"

A cloud slid across the moon, shutting off the only light. Abby could no longer see the woman and could barely see Rob, who was still moving toward the stone chimney. A moment later he disappeared into the darkness.

"Rob?" she called. Panic rushed through her when he didn't answer. *Please God, let him be all right.*

"Rob!"

"I'm right here. Are you okay?" he said and ran toward her. At that moment the moon peeked out from the cloud and lit the place like a street light.

As soon as he reached her, Rob pulled Abby into his arms and held her close.

"Are you all right?" he asked again.

"I'm okay," she said in a muffled voice. Her head was against his chest and she wasn't about to pull away. "Did you see her up close?"

"No. She wouldn't answer and then I couldn't see her anymore. It was as if she disappeared into thin air."

"Rob, that looked like the officer's wife who burned down the fort!"

"Abby, that's only a legend. You said no one knew why

43

the fort burned."

"Well, they can't prove it. But you saw how she was dressed."

Rob turned Abby so he could hug her while they walked.

"Do you have a flashlight in your car?"

"No. Why?"

"We need to track down that woman. Perhaps it was someone from wardrobe. No, that doesn't make sense. She would have answered when I called. Besides, why would someone be out here in the middle of the night when the filming is going on down at Buffalo Gap?"

"Unless she was a ghost."

"I don't believe in ghosts, Abby."

"I don't either. I don't know why I said that."

Rob laughed and leaned down and kissed her on top of the head. He placed her arm around his waist and his arm around her shoulder tightened.

"Let's get you home. A few hours sleep will help us see this in a different light. We're too full of the legends of Fort Phantom Hill to come up with a logical answer to who that was."

"But it was someone. We both saw her?" she asked as they walked with their arms around each other. She felt protected by their closeness.

"Sure. No doubt about that."

"There are hundreds of places she could be. I played hide-and-go-seek out here as a kid. I know every hole under every chimney, every rise, every possible place she could go. If it were daylight, we could find her."

They reached Abby's car and Rob asked if he could drive. Without reservation, Abby handed him the keys. He backed the car around until he could focus the high beams on the area where they had seen the old woman. The chimney of the burned bake house stood there as lonely as ever.

"I wonder. . .," he said, but didn't finish. They rode in silence for a while, both lost in thought.

"Where is the meeting tomorrow?" Abby asked. "I mean, in a few hours? It's already tomorrow."

"At the hotel. Why don't you come over about seven and I'll treat you to breakfast before we meet with Sid. I'll drop the script off at his room so he can look it over before we meet. He'll be the first to leave the shoot tonight. While the crew's packing up their cameras, he'll be sawing logs."

"And Chase, too?"

"He has to take off makeup and change clothes, but he'll be right on Sid's heels."

"Are you usually right behind Sid, too?"

"There are times when I actually get time off while the rest are working. I put in the odd hours when needed. Most of my work is done before we get to the actual filming."

He pulled the car up to the covered entrance to the hotel.

"Thanks for all your help today, Abby. You're a real trouper."

He leaned over and kissed her full on the lips. It wasn't one of those Hollywood pecks on the cheek like he'd given Emily in the trailer. This was an honest to goodness, man to woman kiss. Abby felt it all the way to her toes.

"I'll meet you in the lobby at seven," he said as he climbed out of the car. "Good night, Abby."

"Good night, Rob," Abby murmured. She slid over to the driver's seat, put the car in gear, and drove down the deserted Abilene streets on auto-pilot.

It had been a long day full of unusual events: working for the film, meeting a movie star, seeing an unexplained woman at the fort, and being kissed by a fascinating man. Too many things for her weary mind to process. Once she arrived at home, Abby fell into bed and slept the sleep of exhaustion.

Abby squinted into the sun as she drove east and with her free hand fumbled in her purse for her sunglasses. She gave up her search when she needed both hands to turn into the parking lot of the hotel.

She locked the car, locating her sunglasses as she stuck the keys in her purse. The bright Texas sky above promised another shimmering June day and exactly matched her mood. She had thought she would feel fatigued after only four hours' sleep, but the prospect of seeing Rob again had given her extra energy.

She had sung in the shower and dressed with extra care this morning. She had considered wearing shorts. The movie people didn't dress for success as she'd been taught in college. They dressed for comfort. But she decided she might not have time to change before Sunday school and she couldn't risk being late.

She chose a simple skirt and blouse, not wanting to be too dressed up for the meeting. She would change to shorts later and maybe go out to the fort for the afternoon. Then she would be dressed like one of the movie people at least for the rest of the day.

She didn't want to think about tomorrow. Her little job with the movie would be over and she'd be back at the bureau giving tourists directions. One more week and then she was on vacation. Maybe then she would go back out to Fort Phantom Hill and watch some of the filming herself. Maybe then she would catch a glimpse here and there of Rob.

She shook her head. Here she was acting like a high school girl. One kiss and she wanted more. She knew she shouldn't get involved. He was here temporarily. She was permanent. She had to remember that.

Rob wasn't in the lobby when she walked in. She looked around at the atrium and the lavish potted plants and was starting for the hotel desk when she heard the elevator doors open. Glancing over her shoulder, she saw Rob. He gave her his lopsided grin and strode purposefully toward her.

She had wondered how she would feel when she saw him again—if she would be self-conscious because of last night's kiss. He obviously had no such qualms, for he pulled her straight into his arms and gave her the twin to that kiss.

"Oh," she said breathlessly, when he ended the kiss.

"Yes, oh," he said softly. "That was such a dynamite way to end last night, I thought it might start the day off the same way. And I was right." He placed his arm around her shoulder, in what was becoming his customary manner, and escorted her to the dining room.

"You look great for only a few hours' sleep," he said, making Abby feel grateful that she had gotten up early enough to iron her cotton skirt and blouse. The forest green print complemented her russet hair which she had pulled back with a banana clip.

"Thanks. Did you sleep well?" she asked.

"Almost as if I were in my own bed at home," he said and couldn't have more effectively reminded Abby that he was in Texas for a short time only. At the end of a few weeks he'd head home for California.

Rob pulled out a chair for Abby and took the chair to her right.

"Are you a breakfast person?" he asked.

"It's the most important meal of the day," she said, quoting her mother.

"I couldn't agree more. It's my favorite."

"Actually I don't eat much breakfast," she admitted. "My mother did her best to teach me to eat eggs, but I just can't handle them first thing in the morning. I like an English muffin, then around nine-thirty a diet soda, and by eleven a cinnamon roll."

"Diet soda and cinnamon roll," he said and grinned. "Your logic fails me."

"I never claimed it made sense, it's just what I like."

The waitress arrived, poured two cups of coffee, and took their orders. A short time later their breakfast arrived: Rob's bacon, eggs, biscuits, gravy, and hash browns, and Abby's juice and muffin.

"Change of plans. I gave the script to Sid last night and we're to meet him in his room here at eleven. He's not requiring the crew to be at work until afternoon because they worked so late last night. He got back after I did."

"So that's why the dining room is nearly empty."

"Yes. I thought about calling you last night so you could sleep later but knew I'd just wake you. And this morning you would already be up. Besides, I wanted to have breakfast with you," he said quietly and smiled at her.

"You mentioned that you have plans at nine-thirty."

"Yes, I do," Abby said. "But I can be finished and back here by eleven," she added quickly. It wouldn't hurt to miss church once. People skipped church all the time for less important reasons. That had never been her way before, but this was a special, once-in-a-lifetime occasion, she reasoned.

"Good. If you have no plans until nine-thirty, would you give me the twenty-five cent tour of Abilene when we finish eating? I've already learned the important things; the way to your house, the library, and the grocery store."

"There are a few other highlights left," Abby said and offered her cup to the waitress for a refill.

"I'd like a personal tour," Rob said once they were settled in the car. "Like how you go to work, where you shop, what you do for recreation—that type of tour."

"Okay." Abby headed the car into the sun again. "I take the interstate out to the bureau."

"Sounds like you work for the FBI."

"It does, doesn't it? We have a few things in common with G-men. We get government holiday pay because we work year-round. The mail may not run on days like Columbus Day, but travelers still want information. We get comp days, and I'm on vacation in another week."

"Are you going somewhere?" Rob had been watching out the passenger window, but at the news of Abby's vacation, he jerked his head back to look at her.

"No. I hadn't planned any trip. Just thought I'd relax and work on my next upstairs room."

"That sounds like a paradox, unless you find painting relaxing."

"No, it's hardly that. But it is rewarding. I'm going to have the finest study around." She waved toward the windshield. "I want you to get the best view of the place. Look to the left."

"Ultra modern," Rob commented.

"Yes," Abby said. "This is only the third year we've been in operation. Texas had only twelve centers until this one opened."

"And you've been in charge of it the entire time?"

"Yes. I worked in Austin before and jumped at the chance to come back home and be close to my family. Want to go in?"

"Another time, maybe, when we have more time. Someone's working now?"

"Every day, rain or shine. I work an occasional weekend myself," she explained.

"I'm glad you were free this weekend. What would I have done without you?"

"Probably nothing. You wouldn't have had to rewrite if I hadn't spouted off."

"And look what I would have missed," he said softly.

Abby studied his serious expression for a moment and had to force herself to look back at the road. She took the first exit off the interstate and drove back toward town.

"Here's the grocery store where I shop, and down that block," she pointed one finger to the left, "is the gas station where I pump my own gas. This is pretty fascinating stuff, Rob. Do you want to see where I went to elementary school?"

Rob laughed. "I want to know everything there is to know about you," he said. "Were you a good student in first grade?"

"Oh, yes. And on my first day of kindergarten, I won the coveted 'best rester' award because I fell asleep during rest time. You can't get much better than that."

Rob laughed again, a deep hearty sound. "This looks like a campus," he commented as they passed some buildings connected by sidewalks leading in many directions.

"It is. Abilene Christian College." She turned down a side street to give him a tour and pointed out the new performing arts building.

"Did you go to school here?"

"No. I went to UT—University of Texas in Austin. Being in the state capital is how I landed my first job with the transportation department. What about you? Where did you go to school?"

"Northwestern."

"A little ritzy," Abby said of the prestigious school. "Are you from an affluent Chicago family?"

"Dad teaches there. Chemistry. It was hard for him to accept my wanting to write. To him life is hard rules, black and white. An experiment gets expected results." Rob shook his head as if not agreeing with that way of thinking. "Mom, on the other hand, is an artist. She understands creativity and emotion."

"So opposites do attract."

"In their case, yes. I think we'd better head back to the hotel if you want to be on time for your appointment."

Within minutes they were back at the hotel. Rob climbed out of the car, but held the door open and ducked his head inside. Abby saw him glance at the back seat and then he looked at her.

"I'll meet you in the lobby at eleven," he said.

"I'll be there," Abby assured him.

He waved good-bye and she sighed in disappointment that he hadn't kissed her. What was she expecting? He had kissed her good night and good morning and she would see him in less than two hours. She shouldn't be greedy about those kisses. With a quick glance at her watch, she headed the car out of the parking lot.

At church she grabbed her Bible and teacher's quarterly from the back seat and ran into her Sunday school room. She had ten minutes before time for class to start, and she wanted to have all materials passed out and be ready to start exactly on time. She might finish the lesson before the dismissal bell and she could let her students out a few minutes early so they could go to the church library.

Abby had prepared her lesson earlier in the week and now opened her Bible to the fifth chapter of Matthew. As soon as the students filed in and took their seats, she asked one of the boys to read the section they were studying.

"You are the light of the world. A city on a hill cannot be hidden. Neither do people light a lamp and put it under a bowl. Instead they put it on its stand, and it gives light to everyone in the house. In the same way, let your light shine before men, that they may see your good deeds and praise your Father in heaven."*

"Anyone know what this means?" Abby asked. "Jennifer?"

"That we should do good deeds and praise God."

"That's true. Anyone else have another idea? Malynn?" she called on one of her brightest students.

*Matthew 5:14-16

"We let our light shine by showing others that we are Christians."

"Good," Abby said. She placed her Bible on the podium and walked over and sat on the window sill. "See the light of the sun shining on me? Can you tell more about me when I'm in the light? Or when I'm in the dark?" She reached up and shut the blinds.

"When you're in the light, we can see your freckles," Bobby Joe said.

Abby laughed. "You're right. We can tell more about a person in the light. But this is an outward light. What about the light inside us all?"

Abby looked down at her hands and concentrated on looking unhappy. Her mouth turned down at the edges and her eyes looked dim. "Do I have a light inside now?"

"No," came from several corners of the classroom.

She closed her eyes and asked God to help her with her demonstration. Her mind settled on happy thoughts, then she opened her eyes. The smile on her lips reached her eyes and the twinkle there glowed from within.

"Now you have a light," Bobby Joe said.

"Exactly. When we help others and share our commitment to the Lord, we are letting our light shine. We're exposing darkness and revealing what is right and best. I know you're fourth graders, but do you remember that song you sang in the primary room?" She began "This Little Light of Mine," and the entire class joined in.

"It's not always easy to let your light shine," Abby said once they had finished the song. "It's not always easy to tell others that we are Christians. It's an individual thing. You might talk to one person about Jesus in one way, and try an entirely different approach with the next person. Yes, Jennifer?"

"I asked a friend to come to bring-a-friend Sunday and she said she didn't want to."

"And what did you say?" Abby asked encouragingly.

"I told her she should come," Jennifer said in a matter-of-fact manner.

"Maybe it would be better to ask her why she didn't want to come. Sometimes we should witness to others in little steps and then the giant steps will come."

A few students added comments about talking to others about God. When they were through with the discussion, Abby marched the fourth-graders to the library and had a quick word with the librarian about her meeting with the movie director.

"Go on," the librarian said. "I'll keep an eye on them until time for church."

Abby fairly flew out of the church. She had twenty-five minutes until she had to be at the hotel, plenty of time to dart by the house and change clothes.

As she drove home she talked to God and poured out her heart about the guilt she was feeling and the attraction she felt for Rob.

"Please understand, Lord," she said out loud. "It's just for a little while. This movie business is so exciting and right now my life is monotonous. I won't do anything wrong, I promise. I won't deny you three times like Peter. I just don't want to bring up religion right now. Please forgive me."

Can you ask forgiveness if you go ahead and do what you've asked forgiveness for? she wondered.

"Please understand," she said as she pulled into her driveway.

She hopped out of the car and dashed for the house. In record time she was back in the car in shorts and a blouse and tennis shoes.

She arrived at the hotel to find Rob on a couch in a sitting area reading the newspaper.

"You made it," he greeted her and whisked her to the elevator and up to the penthouse. Emily, without her clipboard, answered the door after their first knock.

"Script looks great," Sid said as soon as they were all seated at a round table. "Those legends should have been in the original book. Makes the ghost seem more real. Even though the viewer knows it's a bandit searching for the stolen bank money, the suspense is there."

"Do you think we should change it so the viewer doesn't know the robber is the ghost who's scaring Callie?" Rob asked.

Sid stared at the ceiling, as if looking for guidance.

"No. This works. We want the viewer to know that Trice is in danger all the time. It might be hard to believe that the ghost would harm him."

"No changes then?"

"None. It's better, it's stronger. How much do we owe you for your time?" he asked Abby.

"Oh...," she said, caught off guard by his question. She had expected him to give her a set amount.

"How about two hundred dollars?" Sid asked.

Before Abby could accept his generous offer, Rob spoke up. "Sid? Really."

"Okay, five hundred."

"Sid?" Rob prompted.

"Seven fifty. You drive a hard bargain. Just so I get my money's worth, I need copies made, and I have other work for Emily."

Rob grinned. "We should charge you extra for secretarial duties," he said. "But we'll go do it. Are the trailers already open?"

Emily glanced at her watch, then handed him a key. "Thanks a lot, Abby. This will save me a bunch of time." She wrote out a check for $750 and handed it to Abby.

Abby beamed. She couldn't believe her good fortune. So much money for one day's work. Well, two days, since she would be running off some copies today. She could buy the wallpaper, the desk, plus the bookshelves for her new study, without touching the money she'd saved for that purpose.

"We'll see you at Fort Phantom Hill," Rob said, picking up the script. He ushered Abby out the door.

"I can't believe you pushed for $750," Abby exclaimed as soon as they were in the elevator. "I didn't earn that much money."

"Yes, you did. The legends add a lot, and I wouldn't have known about them without you. Believe me, you'll earn it before the day's over. Sid will need forty copies of this script. That will take us all afternoon."

"I don't mind," Abby said. Cooped up in an air-conditioned trailer with Rob seemed like a little bit of heaven, and being paid so generously was an added bonus.

They zipped along the highway to Fort Phantom Hill as Abby told Rob all about her plans for her new study and the oak schoolteacher's desk she had been eyeing at the used furniture store. She failed to mention that it was going to be a place for her to write. She wasn't ready to confide that dream to anyone.

"I'll help you with your study. I've never hung wallpaper before, but I'm a fast learner."

"Wonderful," Abby said, thrilled that she would be seeing Rob after the day ended. "Wallpaper hanging is a job for two people."

She parked her car in the empty area designated for the movie crew, and they walked toward the trailer. Rob detoured them by the site of the old bake house chimney where they had seen the old woman. They looked behind the chimney and inside the firebox, but saw nothing unusual.

"Are we looking for footprints?" Abby asked.

"I don't know. I just thought there might be something. A piece of cloth caught on a thorn bush."

"I think you've watched too many movies," Abby said, although her voice was hushed. "There isn't a thorn bush around. But it is spooky, even in the daylight." She looked over the deserted fort. "I've been here so many times in my life, but I never felt a sense of foreboding before last night."

"Let's get this work done, then maybe we can explore some more," Rob said.

They walked on to the trailer and he unlocked the door. The heat inside was oppressive.

"The air-conditioning isn't working," he said as he flipped on the light switch.

Nothing happened.

"That's funny. We have no power." He flicked the

switch back and forth.

"Maybe a fuse blew," Abby suggested.

"We don't use standard electricity. We use our own gasoline generator. Let's check another trailer."

Together they checked the next trailer and the next. Nothing worked.

"I know absolutely nothing about generators," Rob admitted as they walked over to the small trailer that housed the power.

"Maybe it's just out of gas," Abby said.

"Not a chance," Rob exclaimed. "The door's been jimmied." He pushed it open. "We've got to call Sid."

five

"Who could have done this?" Abby asked.

"And why?" Rob added. "And what exactly did they do? There's no visual sign of damage." He looked over the machine in the light that poured through the one window. "I don't know enough about it to try to start it up."

"Me, either," Abby said. "What about a phone?"

"In the other trailer."

They quickly covered the ground back to the closest trailer and Rob called the hotel while Abby waited outside. She could hear his conversation through the open door.

"Emily says she'll have someone right out," he said, as he descended the steps into the fresh air. "It's sweltering in there. I opened the windows, but that's not going to cool off that tin can." He pushed his hair off his perspiring forehead. "Sometimes we have guards on the set. Sid must have thought it was unnecessary out here. We should tell him about the old woman we saw."

"You think she pried open the door and sabotaged the generator?"

"I don't know. Let's walk around and see if there's any other damage. We really don't know that the generator's been tampered with, but why else would someone jimmy the door? And we certainly don't have power right now. If the mechanics can't get the generator working, we'll have to find another place to copy the script."

"I can't think of a copy place open on Sunday," she said, then quickly amended her statement. "We could use my office, although the movie company would have to pay for the copies."

"That would work," Rob said.

They checked each of the trailers they hadn't already entered to make sure the locks were secure. Then they zig-zagged through the ruins, looking for anything that seemed out of place.

"Do you think the practical joke in the bathrooms yesterday is related to this one?" Abby asked.

"What practical joke?"

Abby explained what Emily had told her.

"Dumping some chemical in a toilet's one thing. If someone dumped a chemical into the generator's gas tank, it's a whole different matter. That would cause all kinds of problems. But I sure wouldn't call it a practical joke."

They continued to walk around the fort until mechanics, Emily, and Sid arrived. Rob explained what they had found and the theory that someone might have dumped something into the gas tank.

The mechanics checked that out first before firing the generator up and pushing potentially polluted fuel through the engine.

"It's the gas all right," one mechanic announced. "Look at these undissolved granules. Looks like sugar."

"Sugar?" Sid exclaimed.

"I couldn't say for sure until we test it. We'll have to pump the tank dry and clean it. Take four or five hours."

"Four or five hours!" Sid exclaimed. "We don't have that kind of time to waste."

"Can we get a temporary generator, just to power the semi?" Emily suggested. "It's not crucial that all the trailers have power today."

"Get on the horn and find us something, quick," Sid ordered.

"I know a contractor who has one," Abby told Emily. "Would you like me to call him?"

"Please," Emily said and accompanied Abby and Rob to another trailer. "I don't believe there's a phone book in here. We'll have to go to Sid's trailer."

"I know the number," Abby said and proceeded to dial on the mobile unit. "Hi, Jack. I need a favor," she said without identifying herself. "I'm working with the movie people at Fort Phantom Hill and they're having trouble with their generator. Would you be willing to rent yours for the afternoon?"

"Ask him how big it is," Rob said.

"Needs to power one huge semi, like the ones the big TV networks bring in to cover UT football games. Oh, well, where could we get one? Fine, let me know." She gave him the phone number and hung up.

"Jack's is too small, but he says the electric company has a couple of big ones. He's checking on it and will call us right back."

"Who's Jack?" Rob asked.

"A special friend," she said, although Rob didn't look as if that was what he wanted to hear.

"A contractor, you say? What sorts of things does he build?"

"Huge houses. And some work at the schools, hospitals, whatever comes in. He's not limited to residential building."

"You know a lot about his work," Rob said.

"We've been friends a long time."

The phone rang and Abby reached for it. "Jack? What did you find out?"

She listened for some time and then turned to Emily and said, "He'll be here with one in thirty minutes."

Abby spoke back into the receiver. "That's great, Jack. Drive right up to the old guard house and I'll be waiting there to direct you. See you in a few minutes. And Jack, thanks. I owe you one."

"You don't owe him anything," Rob said in a tight voice. "The production company will pay him for his time and the rental fee."

"Rob? That's an expression. Jack's a nice guy. You'll like him," Abby said.

"I wouldn't bet on that," Emily said and smiled. "I'll go tell Sid that we're back in business."

"Rob, what's wrong?" Abby asked as they wandered back to the others.

"Nothing. Nothing at all," he said and Abby could tell by the tone of his voice that he wanted to drop the subject. "We'd better tell Sid about the old woman we saw last night."

They reported the strange sighting of the previous night, and although Sid laughed at the idea of a phantom, he decided to hire some security guards.

"We don't need anything else like this mess," he said.

"You wouldn't happen to know any off-duty policemen we can call?" Emily asked Abby and chuckled softly.

Abby glanced at Rob's scowling face. "Actually I do

know someone," she said. "If you'd like I can call him."

"Sure. It's nice having someone local who has friends in the right places," Emily said and laughed. "Rob, you don't need to come with us."

"That's all right. I'm stuck waiting around until the generator comes, then Abby and I are going to her office to run these copies."

Abby made the second call. Rob climbed into the trailer and stood beside her while she talked.

"Ted, I'll let you talk to Emily Wilson. She knows all the details of time and pay and how many men she needs." Abby handed the phone to Emily and stepped out of the heat of the trailer. Rob followed her.

"Is Ted another special friend?" he asked gruffly.

Abby smiled. Rob was jealous. Odd, when their relationship was just a passing of ships in the night. But then, she'd felt a stab of jealousy when Marilee had been hanging on Rob at the library.

"Ted's my brother."

"Oh," Rob said with an entirely different inflection. "I didn't know you had a brother."

"I have three brothers, Reece, Ted, and Doug, and one sister, Elaine. They all live in the area," she said and started walking toward the road. "We're very close."

"I'd like to meet them." Rob fell in step beside her and nonchalantly dropped his arm around her shoulder.

"All right," Abby said. "I'll take you around on another sight-seeing tour and you can meet all my relatives. At least the immediate ones. I'm from a huge family. What about you?"

"Just myself and one sister. She lives in a small town in

Wisconsin, not far from Chicago. Married a dentist."

"A much more acceptable profession than screenwriting."

"Exactly. Although my dad has come around in the last few years. It was at first, before my name appeared in any credits, that he was so against my choice of careers. Maybe he was afraid I'd work on X- or R-rated movies. But I'd never do that," Rob said adamantly.

"Really?" Abby asked with raised eyebrows.

"I don't believe in all the junk that gets put in movies today. I only do G, PG, and PG-13 movies. Sometimes those get rough enough."

Abby's opinion of Rob, already high, climbed a couple more notches.

"I've written a letter to the producers protesting *Last in Dallas*. The book was good, but the movie was horrible. Why would they add all that sex and violence?" she asked.

"Money," Rob answered. "They think it sells more tickets. The only way to protest what comes out of Hollywood is to stay away from the box office."

Abby nodded her agreement. The man was full of interesting opinions.

"This place is beginning to fill up," Abby said, glancing at the steady stream of cars turning onto the field that had been renamed a parking lot. "I'll bet Barb will be out here soon to watch the action. And probably my mother. I've seen several of her neighbors out here. There's old Mr. Turner," she said and waved, although the old man didn't wave back. "His place borders the fort. This excitement brings them in."

"Sure does. I'm glad you found us a generator. We need

to get all of Chase's solo shots in the can before Miss Penny arrives tomorrow."

"Why do you call her Miss Penny?" Abby asked.

"Because she puts on airs. She's a small town girl who made it big time in the last two years, but she gives the impression that she's been in the business a long time."

"And you don't like her?" Abby leaned against one of the mesquite trees close to the guard house, taking her post to wait for Jack.

Rob's eyes took on a shadowed look. "I met her three years ago and introduced her to Sid."

"Ah-ha," Abby said. "So she wanted to be in movies."

"Exactly. By then I'd worked with Sid on and off for several years. She made a big play for me so I'd introduce her to the power people."

"And are you still carrying a torch for her?" Abby asked and held her breath while she waited for his answer.

"No. But she taught me a valuable lesson I'll never forget. When I meet a woman, my number one question is this: Do you want to be in pictures?"

"And hope you get an honest answer."

"Right," he said and studied her intently. Abby held his gaze, then glanced at the road as she heard the sound of a heavy truck.

"Here's Jack with the generator." She waved her arms to catch his attention. The driver waved back at her and she motioned for him to maneuver the truck, which had Adamson Construction Company lettered on the door, to the side of the main movie trailer.

"Jack, you made record time," she called to him as he climbed down from the high cab. He was a big man, maybe six four, and big boned, too. He had always made her feel very feminine.

"The electric company said if I delivered it, I could use it. Is this where you want it, Abby?"

"Rob, is this close enough?"

"It's fine," he said, his voice sounding tight again.

Abby introduced the two men who shook hands and sized each other up as if they were in a boxing ring. One in tee shirt, jeans, and cowboy boots, the other in a baseball cap, shorts, and Nikes. Emily and Sid joined the group, and then Emily scurried off to get the men who would hook the cables to the generator.

"All right," Sid said. "Now we can get on with it. Rob, do you have the copies for today's shoot?"

"We're leaving right now to find another copy machine. I'll be back before Chase is out of makeup."

He placed a possessive hand around Abby. "Excuse us, Jack. We've got work to do."

"Thanks again, Jack. Emily will take care of any paperwork you have. I'll talk to you later." Abby waved and let Rob escort her back to her car.

She climbed behind the wheel and waited for Rob to buckle up before reversing the car and driving to her office.

Abby parked the car beside several others in the lot. She nodded to the middle-aged woman behind the counter who was giving directions to an elderly man. Skirting around the other tourists who were gazing at the various displays touting Texas as a vacation spot, she led Rob to the back room.

"We need to get a display up about the filming at Fort

Phantom Hill. I'll work on that tomorrow," Abby said. "Which pages do we need to run first?"

Rob studied the shooting schedule on top of the script and pulled out the necessary pages.

"Forty of each of these?"

"Yes."

Abby set the machine and watched as it spit out page after page.

"Would you take today's script back to Sid while I keep this machine running?" Rob asked.

"No, you go ahead," she said and handed him her car keys. "He might have more instructions for you. I can handle this end and start collating pages."

Rob agreed. As soon as they had the necessary pages ready, he stacked them and started for the door. "See you later, Abby."

"Take your time," she said and slid one sheet from the copier and inserted another. She looked up, expecting him to be gone, but he had walked over behind her.

"Do you need something else?" she asked.

"Yes, I do." He leaned down just as Abby's employee entered the workroom. Abby thought he was going to kiss her, but he merely gave her the Hollywood buzz on her cheek as he had Emily the night before. "Later," he promised and strode out of the room.

"Hello, Sara. Everything okay up front?" Abby asked.

"Empty for the moment. Who's that man, Abby?"

"Rob Vincent. He's the screenwriter for the movie out at the fort. They're having electrical problems, so I volunteered to let them use our copy machine. For a price, of course."

"Anything I can do to help?"

"Thanks, but I have it under control. And Rob will be back pretty soon to help me."

Sara went back to her post behind the counter in the front room and Abby fell into a rhythm of sorting, switching the page to be copied, and sorting some more. She worked steadily, with forty separate stacks of paper mounting around her on the floor, on a desk, and on the work table. After an hour she drank a diet soda then had to sort several pages at the same time as the machine got ahead of her.

Abby glanced at her watch more than once. Rob had been gone almost two hours. There really wasn't much for him to do and she was keeping up with the work, but she would have welcomed the company. She also wanted to explore what would have happened between them if Sara hadn't chosen that exact moment to pop into the workroom.

But what did she want to happen?

"Dear God, show me the way. Please give me direction in dealing with Rob." As usual, Abby turned to God for help when she was troubled.

Her mind still on Rob, she switched the page under the copy plate and started her rounds of placing the finished page on top of each of the forty stacks.

"Does he really need forty copies?" she grumbled to herself.

"Yes, he does," a deep voice answered her.

She whirled around to see Rob holding two white fast food sacks.

"Lunch. Tacos, medium sauce. Did I guess right?"

"Perfect. I'm starved," Abby said and realized it had

been a long time since breakfast.

"I thought you would be since you missed your morning cinnamon roll. Is there any surface in here where I could set out our lunch?"

Abby moved some stacks from the work table to a vacant spot on the floor. Rob unpacked the lunch from the first sack and two large paper cups from the second one.

"Diet," he announced as he pointed to one drink. He moved some papers from the chairs so they could sit down.

Abby changed the sheet on the copier before she tackled the first taco. Every few minutes she started a new sheet so that by the end of their meal they had several sets of pages to collate.

They worked quickly and after they caught up, they took turns adding the new pages to the stacks.

"I met your brother," Rob said. "Nice guy."

"Thanks. Then Ted's going to work out there?"

"Yes. Sid wanted the crowd to see the police this afternoon and maybe discourage any more vandalism. Ted's working now, and he's got a whole schedule of policemen to rotate night and day shifts."

"Ted's been on the force for over ten years. You couldn't find anyone more reliable." Pride resonated in her voice.

"He's quite a bit older than you."

"Thirteen years. He's next to oldest and I'm the youngest of the brood. The first four were stair steps in ages, then there was a long gap before I came along."

"The rest all married?" he asked.

"Yes. And they are all parents, too. My folks continually remind me that it's my turn to give them some grandchildren."

Rob stopped stacking pages and turned to look at her. "Why haven't you married, Abby? You're what? Twenty-five, twenty-six?"

"I'm twenty-six. I guess I'm waiting for Mr. Right, and the men I'm dating now and then are just friends."

"The men you're dating? I thought you said there was no one special."

"There isn't one special guy. I usually date several at a time, but it isn't as if I play one against the other. We're friends," she said and shrugged.

"Did it ever occur to you that the men might not think of you as a friend?"

"On occasion." She thought of Milton and knew she needed to talk to him. "I encourage them to date others, too. And when I think a guy is getting too serious, I end it."

"Just like that."

"What else can I do? When there's no spark, there's nothing." She held her hands out in an empty gesture.

"And there's no spark with Jack? Isn't he one of the friends you're dating?"

"Occasionally. But there's no great spark there."

"So now are you telling me there are degrees of sparks? From a little spark to a great spark?"

"This is a silly conversation," Abby said and took her turn sorting the pages.

"Just trying to understand you, Abby." He stopped her as she was passing his chair with the pages. "How does this rate on the spark scale?" He pulled her into his arms and kissed her. His lips moved sensuously over hers. After a long moment, he lifted his head, but still held her close.

"Well?"

Abby cleared her throat. "Well, that certainly has possibilities."

"For a spark?"

"Yes," she said, but knew she was lying. There was no spark between them. Only flames.

six

"Fire," yelled one of the crew.

"Fire," echoed another.

"Everyone back," someone else called.

"Why are they burning this field?" Abby asked Rob, looking around at the fire trucks stationed out of sight of the cameras.

They had finished copying the script and had delivered it to Sid. Filming had stopped at Fort Phantom Hill and the filming crews had moved a couple of miles away to a location that resembled the land formations at the fort.

"We've been waiting for a calm day. The wind sure blows fierce here."

"I can understand wanting a calm day to burn. But why here? I thought the fort was going to burn," Abby said.

"The magic of movies. Film of the fort will be superimposed on top of the burning scene and you'll think the fort is burning. We don't want to burn the fort because we need the vegetation for the rest of the filming. You know we don't film in sequence. The burning of the ruins is one of the last scenes."

"Quiet on the set," someone yelled.

Abby and Rob stood behind a rope that cordoned off the crowd from the camera crews.

"Wasn't this supposed to happen at night?" Abby whispered.

"Again, the magic of movies. By doing it at dusk, the wind has died down and the crowd has thinned because of hunger pains. By using a gray glass filter, we can make it appear like night," he explained.

"There's so much phoniness in the movie business, I'm surprised you're filming on location at all."

"There's a lot that appears more authentic because of location shots. Buffalo Gap is actually a greater asset than the fort. Having a turn-of-the-century village already built and usable saves us money in the long run."

"Look at the fire," Abby whispered in awe. She stood hypnotized by the flames that shot as high as eight feet. A mesquite tree exploded from the heat. The fire trucks had soaked the ground around the spectators and the crew had dug a firebreak in front of the cameras, so there was little danger of the fire getting out of control. Five cameras filmed the inferno from different angles.

"Cut," Sid yelled.

"That's it," Rob said. "This is the last scene of the day."

"Are you finished, too?" Abby asked.

"Yes. I looked at rushes with Sid when I brought the first pages out."

"Rushes?"

"The film from yesterday. We see it every day. I don't always watch, but today I helped peg the scenes we had to reshoot because of the changes in script. Like that scene you saw yesterday with Chase that caused the rewrite."

"Oh," Abby said. She had learned a great deal about the movie industry and still found the process fascinating. But now her time was up. For a while she had felt like a part of the Hollywood scene. Although this episode of her life was ending, she wanted to drag it out a few minutes longer.

"I'll be glad to give you a ride back to the hotel," she offered.

"What are you doing for dinner?"

"I don't know. I'll probably have a grilled cheese sandwich and start the laundry that I didn't get done this weekend."

"Would you mind if I joined you?" Rob asked.

"You want to watch me do laundry?"

"I'd just like to be with you."

Abby smiled. "I'd like that, too," she admitted. Her heart rejoiced that she had been given an extension of their time together. She had asked for God's guidance. She would trust that things would develop as He wanted them to.

"Hey, Vincent," Sid called to Rob as they were walking to the car. "Rushes at ten, my room."

"I'll be there," Rob answered.

As soon as they arrived back at Abby's house, she started the washing machine while Rob took over kitchen duty.

"Want soup with this?" he called into the utility room where she was sorting clothes. "You have tomato and chicken noodle."

"You choose. I like them both."

When she returned to the kitchen, Rob had set the table for two and was heating chicken noodle soup in the microwave.

"Oh, a real gourmet," Abby teased. She flipped the sandwiches in the skillet, and while waiting for the sandwiches to finish browning, she poured iced tea into two glasses and carried them to the table.

"Bowls?" Rob asked.

Abby pointed to a cabinet. He took up the soup, she placed the sandwiches on plates, and they sat down to a meal made delicious because they had fixed it together.

"What do you usually do on Sunday nights?" Rob asked.

Abby smiled. "I like to stretch out on the couch and watch the mystery movie. Relax before starting out the work week." On occasion she helped her sister with the youth group at church, but she didn't mention that. "What about you?"

"I like to stretch out and watch the mystery movie."

"You're kidding."

"No. Really. I don't get to often, because we're on location. But when I'm at home, I like to relax on Sunday night."

Abby glanced at her watch. "Movie starts in ten minutes. Can we have the dishes done by then?"

"No problem. Do you have popcorn about halfway through the movie?"

"No, I have ice cream," Abby said. "But I can change my routine for once."

"We'll compromise. Ice cream tonight and next Sunday night we'll have popcorn. Let's get moving."

They stacked the dishwasher, Abby put her clothes in the dryer, and they were in front of the TV with time to spare. Sitting on the couch with Rob's arm around her, Abby couldn't remember a better, more contented Sunday night.

She had known Rob for roughly thirty-six hours and yet felt a sense of harmony with him that she had never felt with a man before. But still she didn't tell him about her spiritual beliefs.

Monday morning came early. Abby was tired from her busy weekend and not ready to face the work week, but she struggled out of bed with the alarm and moved in slow motion through her normal morning routine.

Talking with God was a part of her day, but this morning Abby more or less argued with Him. Guilt for not sharing her belief in God with Rob led her to defend herself.

"Just for a little while longer, Lord. He's not said anything about You, either. And if he isn't a Christian, I won't get involved with him. I couldn't."

But aren't you already involved? a voice within her asked.

"I'll talk to him soon," she said out loud. "When the time is right. When I know him better, I'll know how to ask him if he believes."

At work Abby concentrated on designing a display featuring Fort Phantom Hill and Buffalo Gap. With Rob's permission, she had kept one copy of the script and focused the exhibit on it, but she wished she had props from the movie. That thought spurred her to find a cowboy hat and some six-shooters. Who better to call than her sister whose son had a well-supplied toy box?

Elaine was at home and happy to loan the western gear. All Abby had to do was drive over. Since it was close to lunch time, she finagled an invitation and zipped over shortly before noon.

"All right," Elaine started as soon as Abby was through the door. "Tell me all about him."

"Who?"

"Don't play dumb with me, little sister. Brother Ted stopped by last night after he patrolled out at the fort. Come set the table. Just for us. The kids spent the night at Mom's."

Abby followed Elaine to the kitchen. "Rob said he met Ted."

Elaine turned from the stove where she was heating barbecue and faced Abby. "He told Ted that you were seeing each other. Something about cramming several months into a few weeks. What's going on?"

"Nothing, really. We're friends. He's only going to be here for a few weeks, so all we can be is friends. There's not time for anything serious." She opened the refrigerator. "Do you want iced tea?"

"Yes. What's serious to you, Abby? Two years? Haven't you ever heard of love at first sight?" Elaine placed the warmed up barbecue on the buns. "What's his full name? And where's he from?" she asked as they took their seats at the table.

Elaine reached out for Abby and they clasped hands while Elaine asked the blessing.

"Now, tell me everything," Elaine said.

Abby related what she knew about Rob, emphasizing their different backgrounds and lifestyles.

"I want to meet him," Elaine said. "He sounds just your type. Remember, Merle and I were from two different worlds, too, and look at us now. Three kids later."

"But not as different as Abilene and Hollywood."

"Ha! When can you bring Rob to dinner?" Elaine persisted.

"I don't know. I haven't talked to him today. We've

finished the script, so I may never see him again."

Now that she had voiced the words, Abby realized her mind had been unconsciously dwelling on that possibility. Rob had mentioned watching the mystery movie with her next Sunday and helping her with the wallpaper in her new study, but he hadn't said anything specific about seeing her or calling her when she had driven him back to the hotel the night before.

"He'll call you," Elaine said confidently. "Hey, do you think he can get us jobs as extras in the movie?"

Abby's mouth fell open. If even no-nonsense Elaine wanted her chance at fame, Rob had been right about most women wanting to be movie stars.

"Don't look so shocked. Wouldn't it be fun to be in the movie? Do you think they have any parts for kids? Ask him," Elaine said, then softened her request by adding, "Please?"

"If he calls, I'll ask him to dinner here, and then you can ask him yourself. Thanks for lunch," Abby said and rinsed off her dishes and put them in the dishwasher. "Could I have the cowboy hat and guns now? I've got to get back to work."

"Come on upstairs and we'll see what we can find."

They found not only guns and a couple hats, but also a sheriff's badge, a bandanna, a string tie, and some spurs.

"What about a girl's costume?" Elaine asked. "Jill wore an old bonnet last year in the school play. She has a frontier dress, too. Could you use them?"

Abby took the cowboy apparel and the bonnet, but declined the dress. It wouldn't fit in the display case.

A few minutes after she had returned to work, Abby had

artfully arranged her props and stepped back to admire the exhibit.

"Looks good," a now familiar male voice said from behind her.

"Rob, what are you doing here?" Abby asked.

"On my way to the airport. Thought I'd drop in and say hi."

Abby's heart flopped over. "Are you leaving?"

"No. I'm going to pick up Miss Penny."

"Oh." Abby didn't know what to say. "How's your old girlfriend?" didn't sound right. She sure didn't want to say, "Have a good time with your old girlfriend." So she said nothing.

"If you have no plans tonight, I thought we might have dinner," Rob said.

"That would be nice. Just today my sister said to ask you to dinner at her house. Would that be all right, if I can arrange it?"

"Sure. Uh, Abby," he said and paused. "Well, I was wondering if you had time to go with me to the airport."

Abby felt her eyebrows rise before she could control them. He didn't want to see his old girlfriend alone?

"I'm sorry, Rob, I can't go. I have to work."

"Abby," Sara said from behind the counter. "If you want to leave, I can cover here. You really had a working lunch anyway, gathering up all that stuff for the display."

"Abby?" Rob said, all smiles.

"Why don't you want to see her alone?" Abby asked suspiciously.

"I'm a little uncomfortable with it. Will you help me out? Please?"

"How long will we be gone?" she asked.

"Not long. Her plane's due in twenty minutes."

Abby glanced at her watch. "We'd better get moving. We don't want to keep her waiting."

"Thanks, Abby. I won't forget this."

Rob hustled Abby out to the movie's rental car. Fifteen minutes later they scurried into the airport and hurried to the gate where Penny Lynn's plane could be seen circling.

Abby glanced around the waiting room at the crowd that had gathered. A photographer from the newspaper was there along with a reporter. A woman held up a sign that said Penny Lynn Fan Club.

"She's really the celebrity, isn't she?" Abby said.

"Um-huh. I don't want my experience with her to cloud your own judgment, Abby. She's not all bad, but she does use people."

Abby watched the plane touch down and the airport workers connect the loading tunnel to the door.

A few moments later passengers began emerging from the tunnel into the waiting room. Some passengers hugged loved ones, and then a hush fell over the room.

"Maybe she missed the plane," Abby whispered to Rob.

"No. She's waiting to make an entrance. All celebrities do it."

A cheer swept the waiting audience as Miss Penny Lynn stepped from the tunnel as if she had been introduced by a talk show host. She flipped her long blond hair back to reveal a picture perfect face. She waved to her fans as she subtly searched the crowd.

Rob stepped forward taking Abby with him. Penny's gaze locked with his.

"Robbie, darling," she cooed, just like Abby imagined a star would greet a friend.

"Hello, Penny. May I have your baggage claims?"

Penny sashayed up to Rob and placed a hand behind his neck and pulled his head down to hers. She bestowed a Hollywood kiss on him that actually sizzled.

The crowd roared its approval.

seven

"Abby, have you seen the evening paper?" Barb asked.

"I just this minute stepped in the door and grabbed the phone. What is it?" she said breathlessly.

"Get your paper, then we'll talk."

Abby left the receiver dangling, dashed out the front door and back inside, and fiddled with the stubborn rubber band on the newspaper.

"Just a minute," she said into the receiver. "I think I know what this is all about. What page?" she asked as the rubber band flipped into the air and she could unfold the paper.

She saw the picture before Barb could reply.

Front page. Center. Robbie and Miss Penny Lynn in a clutch, with Abby herself in the background.

"Oh, no," she whispered.

"Oh, yes," said Barb. "That look on your face could melt steel. What were you doing out there and what's going on?"

Abby studied her expression in the photo. If ever she had seen a more un-Christian look on her face, she didn't know when it would be. What was happening to her?

She sighed into the phone. "I don't know what's going on. Rob asked me to go with him to pick her up. She sat in the front seat with Robbie and chattered on about old times all the way to the hotel."

"Will you introduce me?" Barb asked.

"Barb! I don't like the woman, and she doesn't like me. I doubt I will see her again." *And I hope I don't*, Abby added mentally.

"Maybe Rob will introduce me. After all, Abby, she is a star."

"She's a jerk," Abby said and immediately bit her lip to stop herself from saying anything else unkind.

"Do I detect the green-eyed monster?"

"Don't be silly. She means nothing to Rob anymore."

He had treated Penny as nothing more than an old acquaintance. That was reassuring. What unsettled Abby was seeing the type of woman who attracted him.

"I think the question is what does Rob mean to you?"

"I don't know," Abby answered truthfully and shook her head.

She liked him. Liked him a lot, but she was also a realistic person. He would be gone soon and she would stay. Her once-in-a-lifetime fling at excitement would end soon. Better to keep entanglements to a minimum. Hadn't she promised God just that morning that she wouldn't let things get out of hand?

"What I do know is that I have to get moving. We're having dinner at Elaine's."

"We? Meaning you and Rob?"

"Yes. And I wish I'd said no. Elaine will give him the fifth degree."

"He's a big boy. He can take it."

"Right. I'll talk to you later, Barb."

Abby climbed into the shower and let the warm spray revive her. For the last three days she had dashed from one thing to the next with only the Sunday night movie as a rest stop. She usually looked forward to dinner at Elaine's—she enjoyed her niece and nephews. But taking a date there was a different story. She knew that from experience.

What had possessed her to invite Rob over? Elaine had been delighted and said short notice was no problem. Maybe the few hours she'd had to prepare dinner would mean she wouldn't have had time to prepare a bunch of prying questions for Rob.

Abby was right. Elaine didn't have many questions for Rob. Her husband, Merle, took charge of that area while Elaine put the finishing touches on their meal and occasionally fluttered around with the hors d'oeuvres. The children were noticeably missing. Elaine explained that they were spending another evening with their grandparents.

Feeling the need for a grown-ups only dinner, Elaine had invited their brother Ted and his wife, Pam. Abby thanked God that Elaine hadn't invited the entire family, which was an odd thought. Her family was number one with her, but Rob was still a very private matter and she didn't want to share him with everyone.

"How long have you been in the movie business?" Merle asked Rob after the five adults had taken seats in the formal living room, which the family never used. Rob sat next to Abby on the couch. The others sat in scattered chairs, but focused their attention on Rob.

"About eight years. The last four I've been the fix-it guy on the set." Rob stretched his arm on the couch behind Abby, but he didn't rest it on her shoulder.

"Is it steady work?" Merle asked nonchalantly, but

Abby knew he was pumping for any information he could get and had probably been primed by Elaine. Abby only hoped he wouldn't ask Rob's annual salary.

"Yes. I've been working with one director for some time and he likes my work. On occasion I freelance a script, but I've only traveled on location with Sid."

"Do you ever use extras from the town where you're filming?" Pam asked.

Rob gave Abby a knowing glance.

"Sometimes we do."

"Will you this time?" Elaine asked. She had entered the living room with a platter of stuffed mushrooms and seemed well aware of the turn the conversation had taken.

"Yes, we'll be using some extras in the picnic scene that'll be filmed at Buffalo Gap," Rob said.

"How will you choose those extras?" Elaine probed.

Rob grinned. "Interested, Elaine?"

"Well, I do have a frontier dress, and so does my daughter."

"I'll find out when Sid is going to give the call for extras and let you know in plenty of time so you can be first in line," he promised.

"Really, Rob?" Elaine said and propped herself on the arm of the couch next to him. "That'd be great. The kids will be so excited. You do use kids, don't you? What would a picnic be without kids?"

"We'll use children," Rob said. "I'm not sure how many, but I'll find out."

"Have a mushroom," Elaine said and offered the platter to Rob.

With the major question having been asked and answered, the group relaxed and by the time they moved into the dining room, there were a couple of conversations going on instead of merely a question and answer session with Rob.

"Sorry about that," Abby whispered to Rob as they took their seats at the table. "Sid could get all the extras he needs by using my entire family. And I wouldn't be surprised if they don't all apply."

Rob laughed. "It's only natural. Movies are fascinating to those who aren't around them all the time."

Abby had to agree.

Elaine sat down and reached out for the hands of Ted and Rob, who were seated on each side of her.

"Rob, would you ask the blessing, please?" she asked in her commanding way that didn't allow no for an answer.

Abby looked at Rob who had bowed his head in response.

"Dear Father," he began in deep resonant tones. "Please bless this food and the family gathered here tonight. And let them feel your love in their hearts. Amen."

Rob gave Abby's hand a little squeeze before he released it.

Dishes were passed around the table and the clatter of silverware overtook the conversation until Merle said from the head of the table, "Say, Rob, that was quite a picture of you in the afternoon paper."

Rob raised his eyebrows in question. "I haven't seen the paper. What was it?"

Elaine popped up out of her seat, disappeared into the kitchen, and returned with the newspaper. It was folded so the photo could be seen. She handed it to Rob.

He studied the picture and nodded.

"Typical celebrity move. A phony Hollywood kiss that goes with the dramatic entrance," he said nonchalantly.

"You must know her very well," Pam stated, although it was more of a question.

"I knew her well at one time," Rob explained. "A few years ago, when she was still Penny Lynn Hoofnagle."

"Hoofnagle?" Abby repeated and smiled. She liked the sound of that. It gave Miss Penny the touch of the common people, a touch she was sure the actress wanted to discourage.

"What's she like?" Elaine asked. "Rolls?" she said as she passed the basket to Rob.

"The typical successful star. Actors tend to forget who they are and act as if they're in front of the camera all the time. It's an occupational hazard."

"Chase seems to be down to earth," Abby said. "Although he's aware of his appearance."

"Again, it comes with the territory. When an actor's in the public eye, he assumes there will be cameras flashing around him. He wouldn't want an unflattering shot picked up by the AP and carried in papers around the world," he said.

"Abby, have you met Chase?" Pam asked.

Abby explained about the impromptu Chinese dinner.

"You lucky thing," Pam said. "Imagine sitting across the table from a movie star."

"Pass the butter," Ted grunted. "I've met Chase Cooper, too," he informed them.

"That's right," Abby said. "Have you found who doctored the generator yet?"

"Not a clue, and I don't think we will. But we have men patrolling out there so something like that shouldn't happen again."

Abby buttered a roll and passed the green beans to Rob.

"I wonder why someone tried to sabotage the movie," she said.

"Could be some kids. Vandals," Elaine said.

"Hmmm. Chemistry students maybe," Abby said. "Didn't they put some chemical in the toilets?" she asked Ted.

"Yes," he answered. "But sulphur tablets aren't exactly known only to chemistry brains. And putting sugar in gasoline doesn't take a mental giant, either. I agree with Elaine. It's some kids out to look smart. If they brag to the wrong friends, we might find out who did it, but I wouldn't hold your breath."

"Are there off-duty policemen at Buffalo Gap, too?" Abby asked her brother.

"Yeah. Since it's a tourist attraction, the Gap already had a night watchman. I don't think anything will happen there," Ted said.

Abby wondered about mentioning the old woman she and Rob had seen at Fort Phantom Hill but decided against it. If Ted knew about it, he would have mentioned it to the others the night before when he had stopped at Elaine's. Abby certainly didn't want to appear gullible. Her brothers and sister already teased her enough because she was the youngest. She didn't want to give them any other reason.

Talk finally turned from the movie to other topics and Rob seemed to enjoy himself. When the discussion touched on local issues, Abby explained names and pertinent information to Rob.

"Elaine, this meal was wonderful," Rob said as they all pushed their chairs back. "After restaurants day after day, it's such a treat to eat a home cooked meal."

"Thanks. We'll have pie later," Elaine said.

"Strawberry pie's her specialty," Merle bragged on his wife as the group adjourned to the family room instead of the formal living room.

"My family's big on after-dinner games," Abby explained. "Charades, board games—you name it, we play it."

The couples decided on a game and drew numbers for teams. Abby, Merle, and Pam opposed Rob, Elaine, and Ted.

"That was fun," Rob told Abby later as he turned the car into her driveway.

"My sister is a nosy busybody, but she means well. And my brother is impressed with himself because, as he says, he's the law. But I love them."

"Of course you do," he said and climbed out of the car. He opened her door for her. "When do I meet the rest of the clan?"

"Are you serious? You want to meet more family?"

"Why not?" he asked.

"Why?" Abby countered.

"Because I want to know you better. And what better way than to see you with your family. They're important to you, and I want to see how they treat you and how you respond to them."

"You're a glutton for punishment. But if you want to

meet them, I'll arrange it. Are you free for Sunday dinner? Sometimes we get together then," she explained.

"I'll make sure I'm free. Right now I'd better get moving," he said and walked her to the house. "With Miss Penny here, we're going to start shooting morning till night so we can get the high-priced actress on her way. She begins another movie in a month, so we start shooting at six tomorrow. We'll put in twelve- to fourteen-hour days for a while."

"Will you be working all that time, too?" Abby fished her key out of her purse and opened the door. She was uncertain whether she should invite him in or not. He'd already expressed a need to leave, so she decided against it.

"Most of the time Sid wants me around for any quick rewrites. When he doesn't need me, I'll work on another western adaptation. This time I'll check the chronology and make sure there's no problem," he assured her.

"Good idea. Well, good night, Rob. Thanks for going tonight."

"My pleasure," he said and took her in his arms. He kissed her with the same Hollywood kiss that Penny Lynn had given him that afternoon.

Only there was nothing phony about this one. It felt very real.

"Want to go to Buffalo Gap with me tonight?" Barb asked. She had stopped by the tourist bureau with morning doughnuts.

"I don't think so," Abby said. She hadn't heard from

Rob in three days. She certainly didn't want to go seeking him out.

"I saw Rob yesterday and he said to bring you out sometime," Barb said.

"Oh, what was he doing?" Abby asked.

"Talking to Sid mostly. They both looked pretty exasperated. Rob's words were, 'Tell Abby I need her. Miss Penny's demanding rewrites.' Or something like that."

Miss Penny. Abby had prayed for her just that morning. Her feelings toward the actress weren't nice, and she was trying to overcome them.

"When are you going tonight?" Abby asked. She wanted to see Rob, and if he was asking for her, it wasn't the same as her chasing after him.

"Anytime you want. I'm running errands today, but I don't want to miss the evening shoot."

"I guess I could go out tonight. Is six good?"

"I'll be at your house at six sharp," Barb said. "See you then."

"Okay. Thanks for the cinnamon roll," Abby called after Barb's departing figure.

Her mood lightened. She had wondered why Rob hadn't called. If he was heavily involved in rewrites and with someone as temperamental as she had heard Penny was, well, that was probably reason enough for him not to phone.

By six, Abby had changed from her dress into a pair of bright blue shorts with a blue plaid blouse, had hastily downed a ham sandwich, and was sitting in the front porch swing waiting for Barb. Just as her friend drove up, Abby heard her phone ring.

"Just a minute," she called to Barb as she dug her key out of her purse. "Phone."

She dashed inside and breathlessly answered it on the seventh ring.

"Hi, Abby," she heard Rob's voice. "I was hoping you could come to the set tonight."

"You must have ESP. Barb just pulled up outside to pick me up. She says you're rewriting."

"Yes. I'll tell you all about it when you get here. We're at Buffalo Gap. I'll meet you in front of the general store."

Abby relayed Rob's quick message as Barb drove them south of Abilene to Buffalo Gap. Barb insisted on dropping Abby by the cordoned off area of the restored western town instead of taking her along to park the car and hike the six blocks back to the scene of the filming.

Abby walked quickly to the general store, but didn't see Rob in the crowd. There weren't as many people as there had been that Saturday morning she had watched Chase walk out of the stone building at the fort. She made her way through the clustered groups, exchanging greetings with the few people she knew.

Stopping in front of the store, Abby looked around again. Still no Rob. She climbed the steps to the porch for a better lookout and spotted Rob between the store and the old church. He was deep in conversation with a man Abby didn't know. Leaving the porch, Abby again dodged people as she walked to the spot where she had seen Rob, but he was no longer there.

Frustrated, she went back to the porch of the general store for her bird's eye view of the crowd and found him sitting on a cane chair by the front door.

"You made it," he said, instantly rising to hug her. He kissed the top of her head.

Abby was going to complain that she'd been playing hide-and-go-seek with him, but his embrace was exactly what she'd been wanting, so she enjoyed it and hugged him back.

"I need help," Rob said. "Miss Penny's being a pain. She doesn't think her character would say some of the lines we've given her, so she wants them changed. The plot's not changing—just the words."

"But Rob, you don't need my help. You do this all the time."

"You're right, I don't need your help," he admitted. "I want your help. Remember, you're a good sounding board. You turn work into fun." He smiled. "Please?" Even his eyes smiled at her.

"All right. When do we start?"

"Now. We're not shooting at the church at the moment, so I'm set up in there." He guided her down the porch steps and to the church in his usual manner, arm resting on her shoulder. It felt as if it belonged there.

"We've been busy," he said. "I'm tired. The actors are tired, the film crew is tired, but we're ahead of schedule, and that feels great. Are we on for Sunday dinner with your family?"

"Yes. The whole clan will be at Mom's. One o'clock."

"Good. Are we still on for the Sunday mystery movie?"

"Wouldn't miss that," she said.

"And your vacation starts tomorrow night?" he asked.

"Yes!"

"Two weeks?"

"Sixteen days, counting the weekends."

"Hey, where're you going?" Barb's voice reached the couple over the din of the crowd.

Abby waited until her friend had joined them. "We're going to work in the church. Want to come with us?"

"No. I'm going to catch the action on Main Street."

The two women arranged a meeting place and time to return to Abilene, then Barb left them to see the filming. Rob opened the door of the church and ushered Abby inside.

The church was tiny. Old rough wooden pews could probably seat around thirty people. At the front was a small table with papers spread on it, obviously Rob's work spot.

"Let's make a deal, Abby. In your sixteen days of freedom, you'll help me with the script, as needed, and I'll help you with the remodeling of your study."

"It's a deal," Abby said and stuck out her hand.

"There are better ways to make pacts," Rob said and kissed her soundly on the lips.

Abby had to agree that he was right.

eight

Friday was one of the slowest days of Abby's life. Although the average number of tourists stopped by for information and there was the excitement of new brochures arriving from the printing office in Austin, the hours dragged by.

At four o'clock, she abandoned all pretense of working and stared at the wall clock. It wasn't as if she had plans for the evening; Rob hadn't mentioned seeing her before Sunday. The crew would be working evenings and Saturdays until the filming was completed so Miss Penny could go on to her next project.

Abby had seen Penny the night before. The actress had come charging into the church with Sid, spouting off about some lines that sounded hick to her.

"This is a western," Rob had told her. "Women talked differently back then, and they acted subservient to men."

"Surely Callie can have a little more spunk," Penny whined. "She would do a few more things for herself instead of having Trice be such a hero."

Sid had calmed her down, Rob had changed a few words that weren't that important to the script, and she had flounced out of the church.

"Ha!" Rob had said once the door had closed behind Penny Lynn. "Penny is being upstaged by Chase, and she doesn't like it." He had grinned.

The hands on the clock had moved ten minutes when the phone rang. Abby reached for the receiver, turning over a half-full can of diet soda. Quickly she set it upright and grabbed a handful of Kleenex to mop up the spill.

"Texas Tourist Bureau," she answered in a breathless voice.

It was Milton Womack. He'd called to see if Abby would like to have dinner. And why shouldn't she? She had broken the date she'd had with him last Saturday so she could work on the movie script.

With the time arranged for their date at seven, she hung up only to immediately answer the phone again. Barb's cheerful voice answered back. She wanted to go to a movie that evening and wondered if Abby was busy.

"Milton and I are going out," Abby informed her.

"I don't know what you see in that guy," Barb said. "Especially when Rob is out there."

"Rob may be out there, but he's only asked me out for Sunday. Besides, Milton's a nice man."

"Yes, nice and boring."

"CPAs are not known for being great wits, but they have their strong points."

"And what are Milton's strong points?"

"He's a Christian," Abby said, ranking that as the most important. "He's dependable." She paused to think. "He's honest. He's intelligent," she continued down a mental list.

"Wow," Barb interrupted. "Important attributes, but there's no zap."

"You're right, there isn't a spark. But I'd like to be his friend."

"He doesn't want to be friends. He's getting serious."

"Don't be silly," Abby said as she picked up a pencil and began doodling on a scratch pad. "He hasn't said a thing."

"He told his sister, who told Marti, who told me, that he thought you were *the* one."

"No!" Abby's pencil point broke.

"Get rid of him," Barb advised her. "Set your sights for bigger game. Like Rob. Remember, men don't know what they want until we tell them."

"Thanks for that very sexist advice. I'll keep it in mind. Hey, want to go with me to buy my desk tomorrow? I'm going to pay for it but not pick it up until after I get my new study ready."

"Aren't you going to watch the filming tomorrow? They're doing the gunfight down at Buffalo Gap."

"I'll have to miss it. Rob's going to call me whenever he needs my help, but I can't see him needing much input from me." She shrugged, although she knew Barb couldn't see the gesture. She wished she could help Rob more.

"Well, if you don't mind, I think I'll go see Chase outdraw the bad guy. I'll tell Rob hello for you."

"You do that, Barb. I'll see you sometime soon," Abby said and hung up.

That conversation had taken all of four minutes. The big hand on the clock simply refused to move at a normal speed. Restless, Abby left her office and went out to the front where some tourists were looking at her movie display. She told them what she knew about the filming, adding that the gunfight was to be the next day. The tourists left with the plan to be at Buffalo Gap for the big event.

"I suppose everyone will be there but me," Abby said to no one in particular.

"Abby, why don't you go on home," Sara suggested.

"Oh, I can't do that. I'm supposed to be in charge here. What kind of example would that set?"

"A human example," Sara said and laughed.

"Don't you have anything that needs doing, Sara? I can help."

"I haven't finished inputting addresses for these questionnaires. It's slow work because people forget how to write legibly when they go on vacation, and they scribble in our ledger. Deciphering the correct spelling is a challenge."

"I'm up for that," Abby said and slipped behind the desk to look at the open book. "Good grief. If I were a teacher I'd fail some of these people in penmanship. Is this a *U*, a *W*, or an *A*? I can't tell."

They debated about letters and signatures and added addresses to the computer's memory bank until Abby glanced at the clock.

"Yes!" she shrieked. "It's after five. I'm on vacation."

"I'll lock up," Sara volunteered.

"Great!" Abby sailed into her office, grabbed her purse from the bottom drawer of her desk, and ran for the front door.

"See you in two weeks," she called over her shoulder.

At home, Abby's enthusiasm knew no bounds. She danced around the kitchen fixing herself a glass of diet pop and headed out the back door to the patio. Plopping down on a chaise longue, she stretched her arms above her head.

"This is living," she said aloud. "No worries, no plans,

no timetables, no tourists." Abby loved her job, but she needed this vacation. In the past month she had fired one person, hired another, worked on numerous brochures, and filled in so that her employees could have vacations. Finally, it was her turn.

She stayed on the patio until almost six when she knew she should get ready for her date with Milton.

Barb was right, she had to admit. Milton wasn't Mr. Right. She had given their relationship time to grow, but it hadn't progressed past friendship. Time to move on. She didn't want to admit that she was comparing Milton to the newest man in her life, but Rob was a more exciting, dynamic man. The spark missing between Milton and her was in full force with Rob.

A shower later, Abby dressed in a yellow polka-dot sundress and sandals. She had pulled her hair back in a banana clip and put on daisy earrings.

Milton was prompt. He had never been more than three minutes off their appointed time in the five months she had been seeing him. That was not his nature. He was an exacting person. She guessed it came from working with numbers.

"You look great, Abby," Milton greeted her. He bent down and kissed her. "I'm starved. Are you ready?"

They went to Mama Cidadino's for lasagna. Abby would have chosen another place, but Milton had already made reservations. Mama was nowhere in sight until they were ready to leave. Then, as if by magic, she appeared at the cash register.

"Abby, you look ravishing as usual," she said. While Milton paid the cashier, Mama pulled Abby to the side.

"You have brought the wrong one. Go back to the other young man. The movie man."

"Thank you for that advice, but I'm not the one asking for dates."

"Don't be silly. Of course you are. In our own way we women always ask. It's in the eyes," Mama said and opened her own eyes wider in a come-hither look.

"Now who's being silly?" Abby asked. "It was good to see you, Mama," she added as Milton joined them by the door.

It was still daylight as Milton helped Abby into the car.

"Would you mind if we drove out by the farm?" he asked. "My folks are in Dallas visiting my sister, and I told them I would water their fruit trees. Those trees aren't going to make it here, but I can't convince my folks of that. They carry water to the trees and hope against hope that they'll have their own apples and peaches."

"I don't mind at all," Abby said. "I haven't been out there in a while." Her thoughts were on how she was going to tell Milton she didn't want to date him any longer, but she didn't know exactly what to say. "How are things at work?" she asked instead.

"Busy. That's why I called you so late about tonight. I've got some clients whose fiscal year ends on June thirtieth and that means some overtime. I thought I would have to work tonight, but I accomplished a lot this afternoon. I should finish up their preliminary report tomorrow morning."

"Good," Abby said.

Milton drove north, and within minutes they passed the ruins of Fort Phantom Hill. Abby noticed a few cars parked there and deduced that some police officers were on guard duty, although she couldn't see anyone among the chimneys.

At the farm, Abby watched Milton load five gallon buckets into the back of a pickup.

"I can help," Abby offered.

"No. You just sit there and look pretty," he said. "I don't want you getting wet or dirty."

He drove them across the fields to a pond where he dipped the buckets, filling them with water, and again stowed them in the pickup.

The fruit orchard the Womacks were attempting to grow looked pathetic. The wilted leaves hung limp from the little branches.

"I think you're right, Milton. Fruit trees won't grow here."

"Yeah, but convincing my mom is impossible. She watered this morning before they left for big D, and yet the trees look as if they haven't had a drink for weeks."

He emptied the heavy buckets of water. At least he was in shape, Abby thought as she stood by a small tree and watched him work. Most men who had sedentary jobs let nature take its course and settle in the middle. Milton played softball, worked out in the fitness center, and golfed whenever possible.

She admired that in him, although she didn't play sports. There was a lot to admire in Milton—as a friend.

Dusk had begun to fall by the time they climbed back into the car and headed south to Abilene. As they neared the old fort, Abby studied the landscape she knew so well. She was about to suggest they drop by and visit her folks when she saw a faint glow a hundred yards or so behind the commissary storehouse, the stone building farthest from the highway.

"Milton, stop!"

He guided the car onto the narrow shoulder.

"What?"

"I don't know. I think it's a fire. Look back there," she said and pointed. "They aren't filming here tonight. Why would someone be burning out here?" This last was said as she climbed out of the car and started for the ruins.

Milton followed Abby as she ran across the field toward the storehouse.

The fire was spreading quickly, getting out of control. But there was someone tending it, holding a bucket in her hand. A woman in a bonnet, a light colored blouse, and a long, dark skirt.

"Help!" Abby yelled toward the fort, hoping to raise the security patrol. "Fire!"

The woman looked up, dropped the bucket, and ran. As she got closer, Abby could tell that the woman wasn't trying to get the fire under control, she was fueling it. She had dropped a gasoline can.

"Get that woman," Abby yelled at Milton. She ran for the gasoline can. "Fire," she yelled again, hoping to raise the policemen who were suppose to be patrolling the area.

Abby grabbed the can and carried it away from the flames. There wasn't a strong wind, but occasional breezes fanned the fire, sending it scurrying toward the main part of the fort. Abby left the can behind the fire line and looked around for something to smother the flames. She saw Milton chase the woman over a rise.

Abby stomped on flames, but her sandals weren't boots, and she quickly gave that up after feeling the heat on her toes.

"Fire!" she screamed again and again. Where were those security guards? She spotted a downed limb from a mesquite tree and used it to beat at the flames, making some progress.

She beat and beat on the burning grass, yelling all the time. After what seemed hours, but was probably only a couple minutes, other voices rang out and Abby looked up to see uniformed men carrying blankets and racing toward her. They also started beating the flames. Someone carried a bucket of water, and the men doused their blankets in water.

Abby's limb caught on fire, so she threw it down.

"Got another blanket?" she shouted at one of the men.

"Back there," he yelled.

The fire had burned around the stone warehouse and was gaining headway. Abby snatched a blanket from the ground and saw that it was a long skirt. They were using costumes from the movie to fight the fire. She dipped it in the water and ran back to the fire.

"Over there," a policeman called, and Abby moved to the far edge of the field where tongues of the fire were shooting off in different directions. She pounded the fiery ground until her arms felt like dead weights.

A siren alerted her to the fire engine zooming down the highway. Her mistake was watching it maneuver onto the field. When she looked back down, she saw a long tongue of the fire had encircled her.

"Help!" she screamed.

"Abby!" she heard Milton shout.

She wrapped the blackened skirt around her bare legs to protect them from the flames so she could make a dash through the fire.

"Abby!" another voice yelled.

"Rob!"

The tall man beat at the flames like a madman, cutting a narrow path through the fire. Abby rushed toward him, tripped on the skirt, and fell into his arms.

nine

Rob carried Abby to safety. He placed her on her feet and hugged her closely to him.

"Are you hurt? Are you burned?"

"I'm okay," she said, her voice muffled against his chest.

"Thank God," she thought she heard him say.

She couldn't pull away from him, it was beyond her ability. She was exactly where she wanted to be, needed to be. She sent her own thanks heavenward as she clung to Rob.

"Abby?" Milton ran up beside them. "Are you all right?"

"I'm okay," Abby repeated. She turned her face to the side so she could see her date, but she made no move to leave Rob's arms.

As the fire engine squirted water over the burning field, Rob walked Abby to one of the movie trailers and settled her in a chair.

"Let me look you over," he said. He took the old skirt she was still holding and threw it out the trailer door. He slipped off her sandals and examined her feet, then her legs and her arms. Her bare shoulders came under scrutiny, too. He wet some paper towels at the sink and wrapped her feet with them.

"I'm taking you to the hospital. You've got some burns

on your feet that may need special attention."

"I don't want to go to the hospital," she protested. "I'm fine. I'll put some ointment on the burns when I get home."

"You're going with me," Rob said, and by the sound of his voice, Abby knew that no argument would persuade him otherwise.

He carried her outside where they saw another fire truck had joined the first one, and together the trucks had the fire under control.

Rob installed her in the passenger side of his car.

"Milton. I must tell him where I'm going."

"Who's Milton?" he asked in a gruff voice.

"He's my date."

"The guy who asked if you were all right?"

"Yes."

"I'll find him. You stay put," he ordered.

He was gone only a couple of minutes before he returned with Milton.

"Abby? I'll be glad to take you to the doctor," Milton offered.

"I've already got her in the car. Her feet are burned. The less we move her the better off she'll be." Rob got in behind the wheel and started the engine, as if there was nothing else to be said.

"I'll meet you there," Milton said in a businesslike tone.

As Rob speeded down the highway, Abby placed a hand on his arm.

"This is not an emergency. Slow down, please."

He glanced at her. "Sorry. Who is that guy?"

"Milton Womack. I've been dating him for several months. We're just friends," she quickly added.

"Tell him that."

"I was going to—tonight. But I saw the fire. Rob, the old woman was there. She started it. She had gasoline."

"The one we saw before?"

"Yes. Same clothing and bonnet. What were you doing at Fort Phantom Hill? And where were the policemen?"

"They were with me. I'm working on a new adaptation for Sid. My computer was out there, so instead of carrying it back to the hotel, I decided to stay and take advantage of the quiet. The policemen were taking a break, having a cold drink. We started talking. The next thing we knew, we heard a woman yell 'fire.'"

"That was me."

"I didn't know that. The security men went out to fight the fire, and I called for the fire trucks. I didn't know you were out here until your date yelled your name. Then I saw you standing in that ring of fire. Don't ever do that again!" he said as if she had done it on purpose.

"I'll try to stay away from fires in the future," Abby said.

"Sorry to snap at you. My heart stopped when I saw your face lit up by the flames," he said softly.

"You certainly moved fast enough for a man with a stopped heart," she said. "Thanks. You saved my life."

"I doubt it."

"Oh, but you did. All I could think of was 'Stop, Drop, and Roll' from elementary school fire prevention week. I should have beat a path out instead of preparing to dash through the flames. I could have been burned badly."

Rob let out a breath as if he had been holding it for a long time. "Let's think of something else. Like who was that woman and why was she trying to burn the fort. Again."

"Again? You don't think she was the ghost of the soldier's wife who burned it over a hundred years ago?"

"No. Of course not. The only ghost of Fort Phantom Hill is in a movie script. I meant again as in it has been burned before."

"We'll have to ask Milton about the woman. He chased after her while I tried to put out the fire."

They did ask Milton as soon as they were in the hospital. He had parked his car beside them and had Abby's car door opened before Rob could kill the motor. He carried her into the emergency room while a miffed-looking Rob held the hospital door.

"Did you catch the woman?" Abby asked as soon as the threesome were seated waiting for her turn to see the doctor.

"No," Milton replied. "I chased her until she disappeared over a rise. When I got to the other side, she wasn't there. She really did disappear. Why do you think she was burning the fort?"

"We don't know," Rob said. "But we've seen her before."

"You two have seen her before?" Milton questioned. The way he said it, Abby had the distinct impression he was more interested in the fact that she and Rob had been together than that they had seen the woman.

"She also disappeared when we saw her," Abby said. "But there are lots of holes under fireplaces where she could have hidden."

"Abby Kane," the nurse called.

Both men stood up, but this time it was Rob who scooped Abby into his arms and carried her into a curtained cubicle.

From their body language it was clear to Abby that both men intended to stay with her. Fortunately, the nurse asked them to leave.

"Thank you," Abby told the nurse when she returned from escorting the men to the waiting room. "Did you put them in separate corners?" she joked.

"Wish I had your problem."

"They're just overprotective because they think I'm hurt. I probably shouldn't be here."

"The doctor will be the judge of that."

A moment later the doctor appeared. He unwrapped her feet and inspected the burns. "Not too bad," he said.

"Just the sides of my feet and my toes."

"I can see. Quick thinking of you to keep them cool and wet. We're going to continue that treatment." He looked her over then gave her some ointment to apply to her feet after she soaked them in cold water for at least four hours.

"Four hours?"

"I would say longer, but you'll want to get some sleep tonight. And it's hard to sleep with your feet in water."

"I can believe that."

"We'll wheel you out, but by tomorrow you can walk without pain. Did someone bring you?"

"I'll say," the nurse answered. "I'll get them."

The doctor took one look at the two men who jostled for position at Abby's side of the examining table and laughed.

"I'd say you're in good hands. Call me in a couple of days if you don't think the burns are healing properly."

Within a few minutes, Abby was home with two attendants waiting to fulfill her every wish. She sat in the living room with her feet in a dish pan of water, a diet pop at her elbow on the end table, the television remote control in her hand.

"Anything else I can get you?" Rob asked.

"No," she said, then, "Yes. Rob, would you go back to the fort and find out how much damage there was and if the woman was seen by anyone else?"

"You want me to leave?"

"Yes. I'll bet Sid will be wanting to talk to you, too. Let me know what you find out. Okay?"

Rob glanced from Abby to Milton. "You're going to let him stay?"

"Not for long. But I'd like to talk to him. I'll be fine here, watching the late movie." She gave him a level look. "Good-bye, Rob."

"Good night, Abby," he said gruffly. "I'll call you later."

"I'm glad you got rid of him," Milton said as soon as the front door closed behind Rob. "He's pushy and thinks his opinion is the only one that matters. He from New York?"

"No. Originally Chicago, now California. Have you ever been to New York, Milton?"

"No. But I've watched documentaries enough to get a feel for the people."

"Since you're so perceptive," she said sarcastically, "then you probably have a feel for what I'm going to say."

Milton turned serious eyes to Abby. "What are you talking about?"

Abby swallowed. *I've started this wrong*, she thought. *Please help me say the right words, Lord*, she prayed silently.

"Milton, I value your friendship. You're such a bright,

dependable man. But, I think it's time we stopped dating so you can meet someone who sees you as more than a friend. I think you'll agree with me if you're honest about your own feelings."

Milton's mouth tightened into a thin line. He stared at Abby for a long moment.

"This have anything to do with Mr. Movie Man?"

"Maybe," Abby said thoughtfully. "No," she amended. "No, it doesn't. I'll admit I'm attracted to him, but had I never met Rob, it wouldn't change this. There's nothing between us, Milton. Although your interests and mine are similar and our goals and values are the same, there's no. . ."

"Love?"

"Not the kind you want. The spark is missing. As a friend, I care deeply for you, but only as a friend."

Milton got to his feet. "You don't have to spell it out for me, Abby. I get the message. See you around."

"Milton, I hope we can be friends," she said and heard her voice tremble.

He stared at her without speaking, then left the room. Abby heard the front door slam.

The late movie had been interrupted for another marathon stream of commercials when Abby heard the front door open. She had not moved from her chair since Milton had stalked out an hour earlier.

"Rob?"

"Yes. Sorry, I didn't want to call out in case you were asleep," he said as he walked into the living room.

Abby clicked off the TV.

"What did you find out?"

"Not much." He sat on the floor beside her chair and reached for her hand. "Sid is furious with the policemen, who should have taken separate breaks instead of both coming out of the heat and into the trailer. We'll probably use fake greenery where the fire burned the ground cover. No sign of the woman. No one saw her but you and Milton. The sheriff took the gas can in for fingerprinting."

"I moved the can from the path of the fire. My fingerprints are on it."

"I'll call the sheriff and tell him. He wanted to talk to you anyway, but I asked him if it could wait since you were recuperating from burns."

"I think you're exaggerating my injuries," she said, but secretly she was pleased at his concern.

Rob dialed the sheriff's office on the phone in the living room. An officer wanted to talk to Abby, and she gave him permission to come over.

"Since I'm still up, I might as well tell what I know now. Otherwise, he'd probably be here tomorrow at eight, and I'm going to sleep in on my first full day of vacation."

"In the excitement, I'd almost forgotten your vacation has started. Were you celebrating that with Milton?"

"No. He happened to call and ask me to dinner. That's all."

"Would you like something else to drink?" Rob asked.

"No, thanks. Help yourself, though."

"No, thanks," he said politely. "Did you tell him there was nothing serious between you?" Rob asked as nonchalantly as he had asked about a drink.

"Yes. He stomped out. I wasn't as tactful as I'd planned to be."

"No great loss. You can't be friends with everyone you once dated."

"You speak from experience, I take it?"

He nodded his head, but didn't elaborate. "What about tomorrow night? Do you have another date then?"

"Not yet."

"But if some guy calls, you'd go out with him?"

"If I wanted to," she said and shifted positions in the chair.

"And Sunday?"

"We're having dinner at my folks and then we're watching the Sunday movie together. Popcorn, right?"

"Right. Do you usually have a date for the movie?"

"No. I don't share Sunday nights. They've always been my time alone."

"Until you met me," he said and looked her straight in the eyes.

"Yes," she said softly. Was this the time she should tell him that she was a Christian and ask him about his beliefs?

"Well," he continued before she could decide, "I'll settle for that, for now. I'll probably have to work tomorrow night until nine or later. Do you want to work on your remodeling later Sunday afternoon? If your feet are better?"

"Sure. I plan to get supplies and samples tomorrow."

The doorbell rang. Rob answered it and ushered in two uniformed deputies.

"Hi, Abby," the younger of the deputies greeted her.

"Richard, how are you?"

"Good. Glad I got sent over. Been too long since I've seen you. Over at Ted's barbecue wasn't it?"

"Yes." Abby glanced at Rob, who stood in the doorway scowling. He walked over and sat on the arm of her chair.

"You're a mess, Abby," Richard told her.

She glanced down at her once fresh yellow sundress. It was streaked with black. Her legs and arms were filthy, too.

"I haven't had a chance to clean up from the fire."

"Let's talk about that," he said, taking out a small notebook, "then we can get out of your way."

Abby told them all she knew—from the first time she and Rob had seen the woman to the events of the fire.

"I've never seen her face—the bonnet hangs too low. I just have the feeling she's old. But she was pretty spry running away tonight."

"We'll see what we can find out," Richard said. "I'll call if we have more questions. See you later, Abby. Take care of yourself."

"I'm going to fill the bathtub with cool water and we'll get you cleaned up," Rob said as soon as the deputies had left. "You do look pretty pathetic."

Abby had to agree with him when she saw her reflection in the bathroom mirror. Her hair hung half out of the banana clip. Her face was even more grimy and streaked with soot than the rest of her, if that was possible.

Rob set her on the vanity bench and hurried away to find a gown. He returned a short time later with a matching gown and robe that Abby had never worn, but had stashed in a bureau drawer. The silky night wear had been a Christmas present that she was saving for a future trip. Usually she wore an oversized tee shirt as pajamas.

"Thanks. I can take it from here," she told Rob. "I'll call

you when I'm through."

Although the water felt good on her feet, it chilled the rest of her and she quickly soaped the filth off and washed her hair. As soon as she had slipped on her night wear, she got out the blow dryer and sat down on the bench to dry her hair.

Rob knocked on the door.

"It's all right," she called. "Come in."

"Let me do that," Rob said and took the blow dryer from her. He moved the hair dryer around her head, gently lifting her hair and running his fingers through the silky tresses. The air warmed up her whole body, but although she felt much better, places on her feet were starting to sting.

"Will you do me one more favor, please? Would you put more cold water in the dish pan? My feet could use more time in the water."

Rob carried Abby to the couch, changed the water in the dish pan, and brought her a cup of tea.

"Tea heals everything," he said. "It's my mom's favorite antidote for pain."

It did taste wonderful. The warmth spread through her limbs, making her feel lethargic.

"You can go now, Rob. I appreciate your help, but it's after one. You've got to be at work tomorrow."

"I don't have a problem with sleep. I can catch twenty winks between scenes. I'll stay until I can tuck you in bed."

He sat down beside her and put his arm around her.

"Rob, I've been thinking about that woman. We need to ask the neighbors around the fort if anyone has seen her before."

"Isn't that a job for the deputies?" He frowned thoughtfully.

"I suppose. But it wouldn't hurt to talk to my folks and some of the others in the area. Just curiosity. After all, you've seen her, Milton's seen her, and I've seen her twice. I want to prove she's not a figment of our imaginations."

"She's not. We may not have seen her face, but she's real," he reassured her.

Rob stayed another half-hour until Abby insisted he leave.

"I'm ready to go to bed. If you'll help me, Rob, and then lock the door on your way out?"

He helped her to her bedroom, and after asking if there was anything else he could do, he kissed her tenderly and went back into the other part of the house. It was a few minutes later when Abby heard him leave. She walked carefully to the window and watched his car pull away from the curb. Then she went back to the living room.

Her feet were stinging again. As much as she wanted Rob to keep her company, Abby knew he had to get some sleep. He would never leave her as long as she was up, but now that she'd convinced him to go, she could get her feet back in cold water.

Rob had put away her dish pan, so she had to refill it. Settling down with another cup of tea and the late-late movie, Abby soaked her feet again.

Her mind returned to the scene of the fire, from the time she had seen the old woman until Rob had saved her from the encircling flames. Like a video tape, she replayed the scene again and again.

There was something familiar about the old woman. Perhaps it was because Abby had seen her on Saturday night. She had been wearing the same light blouse and dark skirt.

Abby's mind zeroed in on her rescue by Rob. What a close call! She could have been severely burned. Reaction set in and her body trembled.

"God, thank You for sending Rob to save me," she prayed. "Thank You for sending Rob."

Much later she fell asleep, proving the doctor wrong. She could sleep with her feet in water.

ten

When Abby awoke, the sun was streaming through the window and cartoons blared from the TV. Her body felt cramped from sitting up all night, but her feet didn't sting at all when she took them out of the room-temperature water.

"Okay," she said out loud. She had a lot to accomplish on her first day of vacation, and she didn't want to be handicapped by her feet. While getting dressed, she wondered what shoes she should wear and finally settled on another pair of sandals. She wished she had the ones she had worn last night, but she hadn't seen them since Rob had taken them off her feet. They were probably still in that trailer.

Over a cup of coffee and a muffin, she made out a list of supplies she needed for her study. Paint, wallpaper, bookcases, the special desk, a painting or two, a desk lamp. She climbed upstairs to the bedroom she was converting and measured the walls and the floor. She might look for an oriental rug. That would add a lot of class to the place.

Before she left for the morning, Abby checked her garage to make sure she had good paint brushes, drop cloths, and masking tape. No need to spend some of her hard-earned money on things she didn't need.

First stop was the hardware store. She had looked at wallpaper before and had narrowed the choice to two patterns. Now that she looked again, there was no choice. She went with the forest green paper splattered with small geometric designs. It would make the room darker, but she was only papering one wall and putting a border around the top. The other walls would be painted a cream color that would show around and above the bookcases.

Second stop was the used furniture store. The old oak teacher's desk was still there. Abby would have to refinish it. She hadn't realized it needed stripping and revarnishing. That would take days. She decided to get it into the garage and start working on it, but to move the desk, she would need a pickup and some strong shoulders.

She could borrow her parents' pickup, but then her dad would volunteer to help her move it. Since he was getting on in years, Abby didn't want him lifting something that heavy.

Jack. His construction company had several trucks. Maybe he would help her. She borrowed the store's phone and caught him at home.

"I know I said I owe you one for taking the generator out to the fort, but now I'm asking for another favor," Abby told him. "I need a desk moved."

"I'll be glad to come help you move it," he said.

"No. I need it moved from this store to my house," she explained.

"No problem. I'm free this morning. Give me half an hour and I'll be there."

Instead of waiting, Abby retraced her route to the hardware store and picked up paint stripper, stopped at the doughnut shop, and then went back to the furniture store to wait for her friend.

As soon as Jack arrived, he and the salesman loaded the desk in the pickup. Back at Abby's house, the unloading appeared a bit more difficult.

"This is really heavy," Abby said. She was positioned in the pickup and was lifting her end.

"Getting it out of the truck is the worse part. I'm holding the heavy end," Jack pointed out.

"What we need is. . .Rob," Abby said as she saw him drive up and park in front of the house.

"Hey, Rob. Over here," she called.

Rob stared across the yard at the furniture movers then slowly made his way toward them.

"Good morning, Abby. I take it your feet are doing fine. Hello, Jack." He shook hands with him and then placed his hands in his jeans pockets.

"Ah, Rob. Would you give me a hand here? This desk is heavier than it looks," Abby said.

Rob climbed up in the truck and positioned himself at the end of the desk. Abby climbed down and directed the movers to set the desk in the middle of her one-car garage. She'd be parking in the drive for a while, but that would be an incentive to work on the desk every day.

"How about a cup of coffee?" she offered.

Both men accepted.

Jack followed her into the kitchen. Rob made a quick trip back to his car and then walked into the house dangling Abby's sandals by their straps.

Abby took the sandals. Once brown, they were now black and even charred in places.

"It's a wonder they protected my feet as much as they did," she said and dumped the sandals into the trash can.

"What happened?" Jack asked.

Abby explained the events of the night before. "As you can see, I'm fine now. A few tender spots, but that's all. I can now swear by the cold water treatment for burns. I soaked my feet all night."

"All night, Abby?" Rob asked.

"Oh. After you left I decided to soak them a little more and fell asleep in the chair," she confessed. "I think all those hours in the water is what's made them quit hurting."

"I could have stayed," he said.

"You needed sleep. You had to work today. Why aren't you working now?"

"I stopped by to deliver a message. Tomorrow is the picnic scene. Sid has decided he wants a crowd to witness the shoot-out, so he'll film it tomorrow, too. If your relatives want to be in the movie, they need to sign up today. And I happen to have the sign-up sheet with me. Emily will be posting it at Buffalo Gap this afternoon."

"Rob, that's wonderful. But on Sunday?"

"We've got to get all of Miss Penny's shots in the can."

"Okay," she said, understanding the need to get Penny Lynn's scenes finished so the actress could move on to shoot her other movie. But Sunday presented a few problems. "You two eat these cinnamon rolls and get better acquainted while I make a few phone calls. Oh, do you want all ages?"

"From infants to old folks. But all must come in their own authentic costumes and be on the set by eight. We never know how long it will take to get good film when we use extras."

"Got it." Abby immediately called Elaine and signed up

her entire family. Pam answered her phone and Ted's family was also added to the list. Abby called her other two brothers, Reece and Doug, and then talked to her mom.

"Sunday dinner's canceled. They'll all be at the picnic. I don't know that you'll need to post this sheet," she said as she added Barb's name, knowing her friend would want to be included. "What about you, Jack?"

"I'll be there. I've got a ten-gallon hat. What self-respecting Texan doesn't?"

"I don't think you'll have any trouble with the costumes," Abby told Rob. "Texans are proud of their heritage and always turn out for our West Texas fair in September."

"What about you, Abby? Do you want to be in the movie?" There was not a hint of a smile in Rob's voice as he asked.

"I think I'll settle for being a sounding board for the screenwriter," she answered him just as seriously.

"Mind if I use your phone?" Jack asked. "My sister would never forgive me if I didn't tell her about this."

"Since the big shoot's been rescheduled for tomorrow, I'll be through working by around three today. Want to have dinner tonight?" Rob asked quietly while Jack was on the phone.

"I'd love to," Abby said softly.

"I'll come by on my way to the hotel and see what you're working on. I could help on your room for a while."

"We'll see then," Abby said and helped herself to one of the doughnut shop's best cinnamon rolls.

Jack hung up the phone, grinning from ear to ear.

"It pays to know people in high places," he said.

"You've assured me of a home-cooked meal anytime I want it. Let me see that paper." He signed four names. "Even my brother-in-law wants in the act."

"It's like that in the movie business. Everyone has a little ham in them," Rob said. "I've got to get back to the set," he said reluctantly. "Anything else that needs moving before I go?"

"No. We've got it under control," Jack said. "I'd like to look at that room and see if there's any repair work that needs to be done before Abby flies at it with a paint brush."

"Jack, I did not ask you over here to work," Abby said. "You're a contractor. Having you look at my room would be a busman's holiday for you. Now, out! I'm sure you have better things to do on a Saturday morning."

"None I can think of. I'll take a quick look," he said and headed for the stairs before Abby could stop him.

"I'd better go get his opinion," Abby told Rob. "I'll see you this afternoon."

"Right," Rob said and walked her to the entry hall. He gave her a brief kiss, then Abby climbed the stairs as he went out the front door. She hadn't reached the top when Rob came back in.

"Forgot my list," he said sheepishly and darted back into the kitchen. He appeared a moment later with the extras list and waved as he exited again.

Abby climbed the remaining few steps. "What do you think of it?" she called to Jack.

"It'll make a beautiful study. I don't see any major problems. Be sure and fill all these nail holes before you paint, and I think you'd be happier with the window sills if you'd refinish them. I've got a hand sander that would get them ready in no time."

"What about this closet?" Abby asked as she opened its door. "I've thought about putting shelves in here for supply storage."

"You don't need the hanging room? Most people find they don't have enough room for clothes." Jack stepped in the closet and looked around.

"Whoever remodeled this house a few years ago made sure there were plenty of closets," Abby explained. "When they added on the master bathroom downstairs, they added a huge walk-in closet. They also garbaged up the stairway by painting it, but I guess we all have different tastes."

"You'd be amazed at some of the tacky things I've done to houses because the owners wanted them," Jack said. "Abby, I could knock some shelves in here for you in a couple of hours."

"Really?"

"Sure. I've got some scrap lumber that will work."

"I'll pay you," she said quickly.

"No, you won't. Well, I guess you could cook me a fine dinner." His broad smile dominated his face.

"Uh, I'd be glad to, but not tonight. Rob already asked me to dinner."

Jack stepped out of the closet and closed the door behind him.

"I thought there was something going on between you two. Where exactly does that leave us?"

"Exactly where we've always been. Friends."

He studied her expression for a moment, then grinned ruefully. "You're right. We've always been friends. And always will be." He ruffled her hair. "I'll expect dinner next week. Deal?"

"Deal." She stuck out her hand and they shook.

When Jack left to get his supplies, Abby reached for the phone and called the mother of one of her Sunday school students. Even though Abby wasn't going to be in the movie, she wanted to be there with her family and watch the new stars in action. Mrs. Hinman had helped her out with her class on other occasions when Abby had been out of town over a weekend. Abby had never given her such short notice before, but Mrs. Hinman agreed to teach the fourth grade class. Abby explained the lesson and the craft project for the next day.

By the time Jack returned, Abby had spread a coat of stripper on the desk and while it worked, filled nail holes in the study walls. While Jack measured and sawed, she cleaned the stripper off the desk and spread another liberal coat.

"Lunch," she called up the stairs a while later. It was almost two o'clock before they took the break, but the cinnamon rolls had kept them going.

"I think one more coat of stripper on the desk and it'll be ready to stain," she told Jack over their tuna sandwiches. "I thought it would take a lot longer."

After they'd eaten, Jack looked at the desk. "I've got my hand sander in the truck. A couple of runs over this and it's ready."

Jack was pounding the last few nails into the shelves when Rob returned.

"Some of the others needed a car," he told Abby when she answered the door. "Can we use yours for dinner tonight?"

"Of course," she agreed.

Rob waved his ride away. "I saw Jack's truck outside," he said, a frown line evident between his eyes.

"Yes. He's been a great help. Come look at what all we've been doing."

Rob followed her up the stairs and admired the closet and glanced warily at Jack. Abby showed him the wallpaper and paint color and told him where she was putting bookcases.

"This would be a writer's dream study," Rob said. "At least for this writer. What can I do to help?"

"I'm through here," Jack said, getting off his knees where he'd been inspecting the shelves. "I'll run the sander over that desk, then get out of your way." He turned to Rob. "You'd better treat her right or you'll have me to pay."

Abby inhaled quickly and, for the first time in her life, her face matched the color of her hair.

"I'll treat her right," Rob promised Jack as if Abby weren't in the room.

"Okay. Let's get that desk sanded." Jack gathered up his tools and handed some to Rob to carry back downstairs.

"Thanks so much for all your work," Abby told Jack after he had sanded the desk. "Dinner next week. Maybe I'll have Barb over, too."

"That sounds fine. Let me know which day. I'll see you tomorrow at the filming." He waved as he drove off.

"You told him you're only friends?" Rob asked as they walked back into the house.

"Yes. And he agreed."

"Good," he said and gave a smile that glowed in his eyes.

"Now, what do you want done next?"

"I want the desk stained, and then I want to go out to the fort and see the damage. My curiosity is killing me."

"Return to the scene of the crime, so to speak."

"Yes. Would you wipe this desk off? I'll stain it." Abby waved away Rob's protests that he would do the brush work. "I have a painting outfit; you don't. I'll be right back."

"Don't laugh," Abby said when she returned to the garage in an oversized white sweat shirt and holey jeans that were splattered with paint of different colors. She carried a can of stain in her yellow-gloved hands. "I cover every inch of skin because I'm so messy."

"Your socks don't have old paint on them," Rob pointed out.

"No. I usually wear old tennis shoes, but they hurt when I put them on. I don't want to spill stain on my feet and have to use thinner to get it off. Might sting."

"Let me do that. I don't think your feet are as well as you're letting on."

"They're fine. Really. This won't take long. After it sets five minutes would you wipe it off with that rag?" She nodded to one she had dropped nearby. "But wear those gloves." She pointed to another pair of the yellow gloves.

They set to work and within thirty minutes had stained the desk.

"This is going so fast. Almost like one of those fix-it shows on TV where they put a deck on a house in half an hour. Most of the time, everything I do takes three times as long as I think it will."

"Right tools, extra hands, things go faster," Rob said,

taking off the rubber gloves.

"I'll change and be back in a flash," Abby said. "Why don't you fix yourself something to drink."

Abby took a fast shower and pulled on shorts and a top in record time. She leaned toward the mirror to apply makeup with a quick hand. She couldn't afford to waste a minute of her precious time with Rob. He'd be gone in a few weeks, and she would be left behind.

Left behind with no one to date. In less than twelve hours, she had told two men she had been dating that it was time to call it quits. Had Rob made her do it, as Milton had implied?

No. It was time they had parted. Usually she didn't get rid of one man until there was another to take his place. Had she been fair to those men in the past? She truly wanted a family. A husband and children. She had given each man a chance to be Mr. Right. But in each case, months of dating didn't create the missing spark. Was she searching for an illusion?

No, again. With Rob there was magic. But she had to be realistic. Rob was not a possibility. Their worlds were too far apart. How could she possibly think she and Rob had any common ground? Of course, they did both like to write, if you could call her brochure research and writing real writing.

Her study was going to be a step in the right direction. She'd hoped she could freelance to magazines, write travel pieces, maybe even write a novel. She would have a wonderful place to work. Even Rob had said it would be a writer's dream place, and he didn't know that was what the study was for. Okay, so they had similar interests.

An obstacle between them was location. Never in her wildest dreams had Abby considered leaving Texas, leaving her family. They were important to her. Texas was important to her. It wasn't just a state, it was an allegiance she felt. A patriotic loyalty. Perhaps her job contributed to that feeling, but it was one most Texans shared.

She had never considered leaving because she had never dated any man who lived outside Texas. The issue had never come up before.

But the real obstacle between Rob and Abby was her Christian faith. Always her dream of a husband and a family had centered on her strong belief in God and acceptance of Jesus as her personal Savior.

What were Rob's spiritual beliefs? He hadn't so much as blinked when her sister had called on him to give the blessing, and he had delivered an eloquent prayer. He certainly acted as if the Golden Rule were a way of life to him, but he had never mentioned his faith.

Neither have you, that voice inside reminded her.

"Are you about ready?" Rob called down the hall.

"Be right there," Abby said. "God, please guide me," she asked as she applied lipstick then hurried to Rob's side. At the moment, her only plan was to spend as much time with Rob as she could until he had to leave. And if he took her heart with him, well, at least she would have a few special weeks to remember.

"I didn't realize so much had burned," Abby said later as they arrived at the ruins of the fort. "It looks like I imagine it looked when it burned the first time, with the chimneys smoked like that. If there were such a thing as ghosts, they'd be here now."

"I know what you mean. Once when I was visiting Chicago, I went to a ball game at the brand new White Sox stadium. It's right across the street from old Comiskey Park. They hadn't torn down the old stadium yet. If there were ghosts, they had to be haunting that darkened stadium while the live people were shouting and laughing around the new lighted field. It was eerie."

"Abby! Rob!"

They turned to find Ted walking toward them.

"I heard you were out here last night. Why didn't you tell Pam this morning when you called? It's not like you to exclude the family."

"I forgot about the fire. The filming was uppermost in my mind when I phoned Pam this morning. Sorry." She patted her brother on the arm.

"You were burned?"

"Just a little on the feet. I'm okay. I'm using ointment on the burns. Have any clues about the old woman?"

"No. Out of our jurisdiction. I called the sheriff's department and had your report read to me. You've seen this old gal before." He didn't say that she had been holding out on him, but the implication was in his voice.

"I thought we might have imagined it the first time, but certainly not last night. Have you asked any of the neighbors if they've seen her?"

"Not yet. I thought I'd ask around when I'm off duty here. Sid's hot about anyone not patrolling the grounds, and I don't blame him. Those guys last night were foolish to leave their posts at the same time."

"Well, we won't keep you from your job. We were just leaving," Abby said. "I wanted to see the fort myself. I couldn't tell much in the dark last night."

"I'll see you tomorrow at the filming," Ted said and waved. "Thanks, Rob," he called after them, "for letting us be in the movie. It's nice knowing people in high places."

That's exactly what Jack had said, Abby thought.

"Rob," she said quietly as they walked back to her car. "I'm sorry my family is using you to get into the movies."

"They're not using me. We need lots of extras. We always hire locals for the walk-ons and the townspeople. If it weren't them, it would be someone else. I'm glad I could do them the favor."

Rob climbed behind the wheel and followed Abby's directions to her folks' house. She had decided she should tell them about her burned feet before Ted did. Abby's mom was home, but her dad was out. Abby introduced Rob.

"I've heard all about your dinner at Elaine's. We're glad to have you in Abilene, Rob. Have a seat." Abby's mom motioned to the kitchen table and immediately produced three cups and a full coffee pot. "We're all excited about the filming tomorrow. I'm still looking for a costume."

"What about the dress you wore last year at the fair?" Abby asked.

"It was red brocade and I was the owner of a saloon. I don't think that would be appropriate for a church picnic. I'm looking for a dress like Caroline Ingalls would wear on 'Little House.' "

"Mom watches those reruns weekday mornings at what, Mom? Ten?"

"You make fun of me," her mother said and playfully

shook her finger at Abby, "but they're good stories. They show good Christian values without preaching."

"I'm not arguing that. It's just that you can say the lines before the actors can."

Rob chuckled. "You should be an asset to the film, Mrs. Kane."

Abby explained about the fire at the fort and asked her mom if she had ever seen an old woman around.

"No. You might ask old Mr. Turner. He's knows everything that's going on out here. I've seen him at the fort every time I've stopped by."

"Have you been watching much of the filming, Mom?"

"Just when I happen to go by."

"Which is at least every day," Abby teased.

"They don't film out here every day," Mrs. Kane responded. "Besides, it's unique. We may never see something like this again. More coffee?" she asked and lifted the pot.

Abby shook her head. "No, thanks. We need to go. See you tomorrow, Mom."

When they were in the car, Abby turned to Rob. "Would you mind if we stopped by old Mr. Turner's place?"

"Abby, are we investigating for the sheriff?"

"No. I'd call Mr. Turner, but he doesn't have a phone. And since we're out here, and it's not really out of the way. . . ."

"Which way?" Rob sounded resigned to the fact that Abby was going to get to the bottom of the mysterious fire.

"Turn left on the last road before you reach the fort. Old Mr. Turner's a bit of an eccentric. He used to own a large place out here with oil on it. Little by little he's sold it off to pay for his collections of glassware, I guess."

"Do you know him well?"

"I used to stop by and see him when I'd go to the fort or to my favorite tree by the pond. Remember the place I would go to think?" Once again she didn't call it her prayer tree.

"I remember my think place, which I haven't been to since that first day I met you."

"Don't have anything to think about?"

"Lots to think about, just no time. Back to old Mr. Turner. Just how old is he?" Rob parked the car in front of a dilapidated farmhouse.

"I don't know. He's old. Rumor has it that his wife ran off with some man long before I was born. That's why he's so odd, I think. He's been alone ever since. Sometimes when I'd stop by he was talkative, and sometimes he'd say nothing so I'd leave quickly."

Abby started to get out of the car, but Rob pulled her back in.

"Get down. There's a shotgun pointed our way."

eleven

"Mr. Turner, it's Abby," she called from behind the car door. "Abby Kane, your old neighbor."

"What do you want, Abby?" the old man called from behind the window. The barrel of the gun was withdrawn.

"Just to talk a minute."

Abby could hear movement inside the house before Mr. Turner opened the squeaky front door and stepped out on the porch. He was not carrying the gun.

"You can't be too careful these days," he said. "There's all them movie people about. Can't be too careful."

"That's true," Abby agreed. She and Rob walked together to the front porch. "There are crowds of people around the fort, but I'm interested in one particular person. An old woman in a bonnet, a light colored blouse, and long dark skirt. Have you seen her around?"

"You one of those movie fellows?" Mr. Turner asked Rob.

"This is Rob Vincent. He's a writer for the movie. Have you seen an old woman, Mr. Turner? I think she tried to burn the fort last night."

"I seen the fire," he said, and shook his head. "But I didn't see no old woman." He continued to shake his head.

"Well, if you do see her, be sure and tell me next time I see you. Will you be at the filming tomorrow at Buffalo

Gap? They're using townspeople as extras. You'd be great."

"No, I don't go down to Buffalo. I just watch the fort to make sure people stay off my land."

"Well, thanks a lot, Mr. Turner. See you around," Abby said and made her way back to the car.

Rob turned Abby's car around, avoiding an old rusted pickup, and headed back down the lane.

"What a character. We should have written him into the script."

"He's a strange fellow all right. Rob, since we're in the neighborhood, why don't we stop on the other side of the fort and ask those folks if they've seen the old woman?"

"Abby, we're not detectives."

"No. But aren't you the least bit curious?"

Rob was silent until they reached the highway. "Okay, Abby, which way to the next neighbor?"

"Turn left and take the next lane back to the north."

The Bensons hadn't seen the woman and were much friendlier to Abby and Rob. They didn't greet them with a shotgun.

"Anyone else, since we're in the neighborhood?" Rob asked.

"One more place, if you don't mind. Turn back on the highway and go right this time. These people might have seen her as they drove past the fort."

Harriet Norton hadn't seen an old woman either.

"You might ask Mr. Turner. He prowls that fort day and night."

"We talked to him. He's protecting his own. He doesn't

want anyone from the movie straying onto his land," Abby said.

"He's been around that fort long before the movie came. We moved out here almost three years ago, and he was hanging around over there then. He's an odd person. I don't think he ever worked at all. Maybe welfare." Mrs. Norton frowned disapprovingly.

"No," Abby corrected her. "He struck oil long ago and then started selling off his land. He buys glassware. His house is full of it. Some rooms have boxes packed to the ceiling. There's probably some very valuable antique glass in there, and he guards it. Well, thanks a lot for the information. If you see an old woman, would you call me?"

They left Mrs. Norton's and Rob stopped at the end of the lane.

"Where to now? Any other neighbors?" he asked.

"No, I'll admit defeat. It's just got me stumped. I'm ready to go home."

"Do you have a membership at a video rental?" Rob asked.

"Yes. You want to get a movie?"

"I thought we might watch one after dinner. We may miss the mystery movie tomorrow night if the shooting takes too long. Sometimes with extras it takes forever."

Abby gave directions and let Rob pick out the movie. She was surprised at his choice, a World War II flick.

"What about dinner?" he asked when they were back in the car. "Do we need to change?"

"Why don't we order in a pizza later and have an

evening at home," Abby suggested.

"That suits me just fine."

They started the movie when they reached Abby's place. Sitting next to Rob on the couch, Abby paid more attention to him than she did to the beginning credits, until Rob asked her to watch a certain part.

"Have you seen this movie before?"

"A few times. Read this." He pointed to the credits on the screen.

"Screen adaptation by Rob Vincent. Wow! Why didn't you tell me?"

"It was my longest movie. Sid's only epic film. It didn't do great at the box office, but I've always liked it, and I wanted you to see it."

"Where was it filmed? Did you go on location?"

"All filmed in California. On sets and in the mountains. Problem is the state is getting so populated, there aren't many places to film. It's easy to make highways look like rivers in movies, but it's hard to disguise houses that dot the landscape. I think that's why Sid started going on location."

Rob told Abby about the different scenes as they came on screen, how they were filmed, and how they differed from the book.

"Have you ever thought of writing an original screenplay?" Abby asked when the movie was over.

"That's what I want to do. Adapting is good work and it's taught me a lot, but I'd like to try my own ideas."

"Do you have one in mind?" Abby tucked her legs beneath her and turned on the couch so she could look at

Rob.

"I like history and a lot of my work has been in westerns. I know it's genre stuff, but it might be best to start on something I know fairly well. It doesn't hurt that I know and like Sid. In this business, it's a who-you-know world."

"When can you start? Aren't you already adapting a novel for him? The one you were working on last night at the fort?"

Rob nodded. "But it's so well written, the script will follow the book at times almost line for line. I should have the first draft done before the Fort Phantom Hill movie's in the can."

"Then you can start on your own. Will you do a book or a script?"

"I don't know. While we're having true confessions, why do you need a study? Do you have some writing plans in the wings?"

Abby jumped up from the couch and paced in front of him. "I'd like to write," she finally said. "I don't know if I can and I haven't told anyone. Oh, I write the brochures at work, but they follow a specific pattern. I'd really like to write a novel.

"I know, I know," she said before he could interrupt her, "everyone says that. Everybody has a novel in them. That's why I haven't told anyone. I thought I'd do it, market it, then shout it from the rooftops if I'm lucky enough to sell it."

"I wasn't going to say that," Rob said, getting up from the couch and grabbing her hands. "I've already seen the way your mind works—logical, pragmatic. You can plot—

you showed that when we worked on this movie script—
and I think that's the hardest part. Once you get a good
story, you can tell it. I have every faith in you. I say go for
it."

"Really?" Abby asked, her eyes wide.

"Absolutely," Rob encouraged her. "You can do it.
You're determined, and that's half the battle."

They ordered the pizza. When it came, they sat across
from each other at the kitchen table and ate and talked
more about their dreams. Abby stuck the extra pizza in the
refrigerator and together they walked upstairs to look over
the study.

"I know a person doesn't need a special room to write
in, but I thought if I had a place of my own, a place to hide
away, I could really be productive."

"I'm sure it will help. It's like your thinking tree out by
that pond. Whenever you went there, you automatically
fell into your inner feelings. Right?" Rob asked.

"Yes," Abby said and thought this was an ideal opportunity to tell him she called it her prayer tree, but she
hesitated and he continued, caught up in the excitement of
her new study.

"It'll be the same way here. As soon as you come in,
you'll get in the writing mode and start thinking cre-
atively. Some days you'll be very productive, and some
days little will come. But a place for writing alone will start
the process."

Abby opened the closet doors. "The shelves look great,"
she said. "I need to stain them. I can see envelopes, extra
pens, and paper in here."

"What about a computer? You really ought to start out on one. It makes rewriting a breeze."

"I could probably swing that. Since Sid paid me so well for the historical advice, I'm using that money for this room. What I had already saved for this project could go for a computer."

"They're getting reasonably priced now, and many stores give good prices on word processing programs when you're buying a complete system." He hugged her to him.

Abby could still feel that hug much later after she took Rob back to his hotel. The spark was there, no denying that. It was a feeling of shared goals and special glances, of confided dreams and goals. If was a feeling she could easily get used to, even though she knew it was foolish. She had been dishonest with him. He knew only one side of her, not the whole person. But did it really matter? He would be leaving soon.

By six o'clock the next morning, Abby was decked out in her painting gear and was staining the shelves in the closet. Then she put the first coat of polyurethane on the desk. By a quarter till eight she was on her way to the family reunion at Buffalo Gap.

One hundred thousand people lived in Abilene and at least half of them were on location, she thought as she searched and searched for a place to park. She ended up walking a mile back to the western village. She should have arranged to meet her family by a landmark, but she hadn't thought of that.

"Hey, Abby!" She heard her name called and looked

around until she saw her dad hurrying toward her. He wore chaps, boots, spurs, bandanna, and cowboy hat, and looked every bit the part of a rancher.

"Where's Mom?"

"Over yonder," he said and nodded toward a clump of trees before the actual village began. "We've been waiting for you so we could have our service."

Abby nodded. Their tradition had started long ago on family vacations. Away from their church and community, the Kanes would hold their own Sunday service. Her father always began the service by reading Matthew 18:20: "For where two or three come together in my name, there am I with them."

This time was no exception. Abby and her father joined the rest of the family by the grove of trees away from the hustle of the movie filming. He recited the verse and asked each person to tell one thing he or she was thankful for that day.

When it was Abby's turn, she said she was thankful for her new friend. It was all she could think of. Rob dominated her mind. Although she didn't mention him by name, she noticed Ted and Elaine exchange a knowing glance.

Mr. Kane closed the short service with a prayer asking for God to guide them all through the day.

"Amen," several of the grown-ups murmured at the end of the prayer.

"Where do we go?" Mr. Kane asked Abby.

"I'll see what I can find out," Abby answered. "Stay put so I can find you again."

Although the village was roped off, Abby slipped underneath the barrier and headed for the general store, which had served as her vantage point before. This time she spotted several familiar faces of the crew, but no Rob or Emily. She climbed down from the porch and made her way to the church. There she found Rob, Sid, Chase, and a host of other movie personnel she hadn't met.

Rob spotted her and strode quickly to her side. "Ever see such a disorganized mess? It's always like this when we bring in the extras."

"Where does my family go?"

"Main Street is the first scene. We're going to start assembling the hundred extras there. The rest of the crowd will have to wait outside the village, so they won't get to see much today. It's just too small to hold everybody."

"Then, my family—"

"Take them to the north side of the General Store. We'll form a line there. When you get them organized, come back here and give me a hand, okay?"

"Okay," Abby said and zig-zagged her way back to her family. She huddled them together and guided them to the general store where Emily now sat at a table, trusty clipboard in hand.

"Line up here, and as soon as I mark off your name and you sign a release form, go to Main Street. The first ones through stay in front of the saloon," Emily told the extras.

"I'll see you all later," Abby called and threaded her way back to the church.

The group in the church had thinned a bit. Chase was absent, but Penny had taken his place.

"I just don't think Callie would stand there and allow the man she loves to shoot it out in a gunfight."

"What would she do?" Rob asked, an edge of impatience in his voice.

"If she runs in the way, she could risk being shot herself," Abby inserted. "Otherwise, she could just scream, which isn't her character. Letting her man be a man might be more her style."

Penny turned on Abby. "And you're the great writer now?"

Abby shot a glance at Rob. Surely he hadn't told Penny, of all people, about her dream. He gave a barely perceptible shake of his head, telling her he hadn't betrayed her secret.

"Think about Callie. Think about the times. A gunfight wasn't an everyday occurrence, but it was a part of the West. It would strip Trice of courage if Callie saved the day," Abby told the actress.

"Callie gets her moment out at the fort," Sid said. "This is Trice's time. The spotlight is shared, Penny. Don't worry, you're going to come out of this movie as a strong heroine." He dismissed her and turned to talk to a cameraman.

Penny gave Abby a killing look and flounced out of the church.

"Sorry," Abby said. "I've had enough of her."

"I think we all have," Rob said. "I don't know why she's being so difficult. Well, what I need from you today is crowd control. Since your family and friends make up half the extras, you get to be the assistant director, of sorts, and keep them in place and in character. I have a diagram of where we want different numbers of people. Keep your group on the north side of Main Street, but scatter them along the sidewalks. Got it?" He handed her a diagram.

"Got it. Where's the picnic?" she asked, looking at the paper.

"It's outside the village, under that grove of trees. We'll have to superimpose the church building onto the film. There's not room enough for all the people."

"Okay. I'll see you later," she said and walked toward Main Street to corral her family.

Chase Cooper fell in step with her at the livery stable.

"Rob tells me this film stars your relatives," he said and laughed. "But not you?"

"Not me."

He put his arm around her in Rob's customary manner. "You're a wise woman, Abby," he said enigmatically.

"Abby!" She recognized Elaine's voice.

"Chase, do you have a minute to meet my family?"

"Sure," he said and smoothed back his hair in an automatic gesture.

Abby steered him toward the group and introduced him to every sibling, in-law, niece, and nephew. Chase shook hands with each one.

"I can see where Abby gets her beauty," he told Mrs. Kane, who nearly swooned. "I've got to go. It was a pleasure to meet you all," he said. "See you around, Abby."

"He's wonderful," said Mrs. Kane.

"He's a nice guy," Abby agreed. "Now. I have a chart

of groupings. Why don't we keep each family together as a unit, so it'll look more real. Ted, Pam, get the kids over here and stay around this hitching post. Don't pose as if it's a studio portrait. Someone's going to get shot here, and you're going to see it."

This directing could be fun, she decided, as she placed people around and gave them motivational speeches. Rob hadn't really asked for that. But she was determined that her folks were going to be the best extras ever in a movie.

Main Street was beginning to fill up. She could see members of the movie crew grouping people just as she was.

"Hi, Barb," Elaine called. "Join us, if Abby'll let you."

"You in charge here?" Barb asked as she hurried up to the group. She wore a royal blue satin sheath with a big bow in back. "Isn't this exciting?"

"We'd better call you Miss Kitty. I think you should stand by the door to the saloon, as if you'd just come out to see what's going on. Matter of fact, why don't you push the saloon door open and walk out when the camera pans this way."

"Abby, you sound like a pro," Sid said.

"Oh," Abby said, embarrassed. She hadn't known he was nearby.

"I'll have to watch out for my job," Sid joked. "This grouping's fine. And I agree with your placement of the saloon girl." He turned to Barb. "Stand inside the door. When you see the red light go on above that camera," he pointed across the street, "walk out and stand by this post. Don't look at the camera. Look down the street at the

gunfighters. Run out to Trice when he shoots the bad guy."
Sid moved on to the next group and rearranged a few
people, then made his way down the street, giving directions as he went.

"Everybody know what they're doing?" Abby asked.

Cries of "Yeah, yeah," and "Yes, Abby," greeted her.

The novice actors waited in the sun, as it climbed higher
and higher. When Sid finally called "quiet on the set,"
silent anticipation fell over the costumed extras.

Abby slipped inside the saloon and stood by the window
so she could watch the action but not be seen.

"Cameras. Action," Sid called.

Barb swung her hips gracefully as she exited the saloon.
Abby could see Trice stepping off paces in the dusty street,
then slowly turn around. She was spellbound, watching the
drama unfold. Other members of her family had their
mouths hanging open. Elaine put her hand over her
daughter's eyes.

Two shots rang out almost simultaneously. Trice dropped
to the ground.

Abby screamed.

twelve

"Trice," Abby screamed again and ran out of the saloon. She knew the script. She knew the other man was to fall down, not Chase. Something was wrong.

Something was very wrong. Townspeople were gathered around the bad guy and Chase was surrounded, too. Something stopped Abby from running into the street. She stood rooted to the wooden sidewalk and watched Chase Cooper stand up, replace his gun in his holster, and then she noticed the camera lights were still on and the cameras rolling.

Darting into the saloon again, she plastered herself against a wall, breathing deeply. Unless she missed her guess, she had just screwed up the first take. Rob must have changed the script a little and had Chase dive for the ground as he fired.

How could she have been so stupid? Her entire family had witnessed her mistake. She edged over to the window and peeked out. Nobody was laughing. They were still milling around in the street, lights were still on above the cameras.

"Cut" Sid's voice boomed over a portable microphone. "That was excellent. We're going to do it once more, just to make sure we had every angle covered. Back to your original positions, please."

Barb pushed her way through the swinging doors. Rob followed behind her.

"That was incredible," Barb said. "I really felt as if we were watching a gunfight."

"I thought so, too," Abby admitted.

Rob laughed. "I heard you shout 'Trice.' Are you trying to get in the movie after all?"

"Did I say 'Trice,' and not 'Chase?'"

"That's right."

"Good. Oh, Rob, you should have told me you changed that scene. I could only see this end of the street and I thought Chase was hurt."

"I did, too," Barb said. "I thought they'd both been shot."

"Quiet on the set," Sid ordered, then a moment later, "Cameras. Action."

Barb waltzed through the doors, leaving Rob and Abby alone. One on each side of the window, they watched a repeat of the scene.

"The first one's usually the best, the extras don't know what to expect and their expressions are genuine—if the real actors don't screw up. But I've seen it take over twenty takes to get everything right. We're lucky today."

"Cut. Perfect," Sid announced. "All extras to the grove of trees outside the village."

The crowd grew noisy as they discussed their morning's work. Abby slipped in with her family, introducing Rob to those he hadn't met.

"I've got to check back with Sid. He may want to view rushes while the extras get situated. If we need any part of the gunfight reshot, we can get it before anyone leaves. I'll meet you later at the church."

Abby's family progressed with the other extras out of the village to the grove of trees, where the crew had been busy. Tables made from lumber resting on barrels were arranged in a long row. Blankets were spread out in a seemingly haphazard way, but Abby knew their positions had been carefully organized to present a balanced picture.

"Were we supposed to bring food for this picnic?" Abby's mom asked as they watched the crew stretch mismatched tablecloths over the boards and place platters of chicken on them.

"No. I asked Rob about that last night and he said the Colonel was providing it. They've ordered fried chicken, biscuits, and potato salad from Kentucky Fried Chicken. Another place is providing some hams and sweet potatoes. They were afraid they'd have pop cans and potato chip bags if they asked people to bring food. All the extras will get to eat whatever they pick up for the scene and there will be plenty for everyone after the shoot."

"Where do we go, boss?" Elaine asked.

"I'm not sure. Oh, look at all the pies," Abby said as a van pulled up and was being unloaded.

Emily had set up her card table and held a portable mike. "We only need seventy people for the picnic," she said. "As I call your name, come over here and get in line for your instructions."

Three men processed the extras. Each extra was told where to get in the food line. Some were told to go ahead

and fill their plates. By the time Sid and the actors joined
the group, half the extras were on the ground holding food.

"Excellent." Sid had the mike now. "I want you to carry
on conversations in muted tones. Make up dialogue to fit
your part. None of it will be on the soundtrack, just a dull
hum from the crowd. We must hear the voices of our
actors. You all know your stations. You may start eating
now. Those behind the scenes, quiet. Cameras. Action."

The cameras rolled for quite some time before Trice and
Callie strolled to the end of the line. The cameras followed
them getting their food and walking to a blanket a few
yards away from the rest of the crowd.

The main actors said a few words, then Trice strolled
back to the table to get pie for himself and Callie. He and
a few other actors spoke by the table. The cameras
continued to roll during the entire time the townspeople
ate.

Abby restlessly shifted from foot to foot. Barb stood
next to her; her flamboyant costume didn't allow her to be
part of the church picnic. All of Abby's family were in the
scene, and her stomach growled as she watched them eat.

"Cut. That's a print," Sid said. "Okay, lunch break,
everybody."

The rest of the extras crowded in line as more food and
this time paper plates and plastic forks were brought to
them. Barb and Abby filled their plates and joined the
Kane family.

"This is the most exciting thing that ever happened to
me," Elaine said. "When will the movie be released? I
think they took a lot of footage of me."

"Right before Christmas, I think," Abby said. "You can't second guess what will be in the movie. Rob told me that over half the film ends up on the cutting room floor."

The crew and extras had all been fed and were milling around when Sid appeared again.

"Attention. This is the best extras filming I've ever had. Every scene was good and we've got plenty of footage. Thanks for your fine work. We'll be sending you complimentary passes to the theater where *The Ghost of Fort Phantom Hill* will premiere in December. Thanks."

A cheer went up.

"What camaraderie," Barb exclaimed. "It's as if we've been working together for weeks."

"It's been great," Ted said. "Thanks, Abby."

"Yeah, thanks, Aunt Abby," her niece told her, and others echoed those words as they left the area.

"You're welcome," Abby said. "I'll see you all later."

"You meeting Rob?" Elaine asked.

"Yes."

"I'll call you," her sister promised, and Abby knew she would be hearing a recap of the day's activities for weeks or months to come.

"I can't thank you enough for today," Abby told Rob as he prepared to leave her house. They had watched the mystery movie together and eaten popcorn.

"You've thanked me. Your mother thanked me, your sister thanked me. But in Hollywood we let actions speak louder than words. Come here."

He pulled her close and leaned his head down to hers, but he didn't kiss her. Was this her clue to be the initiator?

Abby pecked him on the lips.

"Now that wasn't a proper thank you," he said and laughed.

She kissed him again, and this time she knew she had achieved the intense Hollywood kiss. It evoked the same emotion in her as the kisses she had only seen on screen.

Rob must have felt the same, for after she had pulled back, he initiated one of his own.

"We start filming again early tomorrow. Probably be through by six. May I take you to dinner?"

"Great."

"Sevenish, unless I call you."

She nodded. "Good night, Rob."

Abby's first week of vacation fell into a pattern. During the daylight hours, she worked hard on her new room. She painted the ceiling and walls, refinished the woodwork, and put coat after coat of polyurethane on her new desk. Barb helped her wallpaper. During the evenings, she saw Rob.

Monday night they went out to eat; Tuesday and Wednesday evenings they ate at her house, sharing the cooking duties. They discussed the day's script changes and problems Rob was having with the new adaptation, but Rob didn't really need her help. As he had told her, he just wanted her around. Abby found she didn't need his help on her room either, she just wanted him around.

Thursday evening Rob and Abby drove out to the Kane ranch and saddled two horses. Abby took Rob on her favorite trails and rode over to her prayer tree across from the fort.

"You can see for miles from here," Rob said as their mounts climbed a small ridge. They watched the sky change colors in a brilliant summer sunset.

"I know. A big Texas sky, land that stretches forever, the cactus, the mesquite trees, the wind. There's something special about this place that gets in your blood," Abby said.

Rob pushed his Cubs baseball cap back on his head. "I need a cowboy hat and some boots," he said, "so I can fit in."

"Not necessary," Abby said and laughed. "It's a feeling inside. It doesn't have to show on the outside."

She immediately sombered as she thought that there were some feelings, like Christian love, that should show on the outside. She turned to Rob. Now was the time to tell him that she was a Christian. But he had ridden over to a mesquite tree and was reaching for some mistletoe. She sighed with relief that the moment of truth had passed.

No, the voice inside her said. *Don't delay it any longer*.

"Rob," Abby said, surprised to hear her own voice.

He rode back to her side.

"I think God threw away the mold after he created Texas, don't you?" She started the conversation in as normal a voice as she could muster.

"I believe He did," Rob agreed.

Abby looked down at the ground. "Rob, I've not been totally honest with you," she said.

"You said there was no one special in your life," Rob

said. "But there is?" His question was more an accusation.

"Yes, there is, but it's not what you're thinking."

"Who, then?"

"God." She looked up and saw the questioning look on his face. "I'm a Christian, and I didn't tell you. I didn't want to alienate you and the Hollywood life-style."

He didn't say anything, so she continued, looking at the sky this time. She couldn't look at him and see that her time with him was over.

"I wanted some excitement, something different in my life. And you came along with a whole other world, and I didn't want to risk not being a part of it."

"And you thought a Christian couldn't be a part of the movie industry?"

She looked at him and saw that he was actually smiling.

"Abby, I gave my life to Christ when I was eleven years old, and I've never regretted it."

"But you never said a word."

"Nor did you, until now. I saw your Bible and quarterly in your car the other day, and I figured your important engagement was at church. But if you didn't want to talk about it, I wasn't going to ask you. I've found that many times I alienated others by forcing my opinions about God on them. I pushed them against a wall, and instead of coming back with me, they climbed over it."

"So you don't talk about your religion around Sid or Emily or Miss Penny?" Abby's mount danced around and she pulled on the reins to bring it under control.

"I know them. They're well aware of where I stand. Emily is also a Christian and Sid is searching. Miss Penny and I differed on that all important issue, so it was inevitable that we wouldn't make it as a couple."

Abby tightened the reins on her horse. "Whoa, Buttermilk, whoa. What's wrong with you?" Out of the corner of her eye, Abby saw movement.

"Rob, this way, now," she said in a calm voice and urged Buttermilk forward with a steady pace.

Rob slacked the reins and his mount followed Buttermilk.

"What is it, Abby?"

"There's a rattler back on that pile of rocks. Buttermilk was watching it, and I was afraid she was going to aggravate it. Snakes won't bother you unless they feel threatened."

"We're going to leave it back there?"

"It's one of God's creatures. It has a purpose for living, too." How free Abby felt now that she could express her opinion. Where before she had consciously left God out of her daily conversation, now she let Him back in.

"I guess you're right," Rob said. "This is a vast country. Surely there's room for all of us."

As they rode back to the fort, Abby questioned Rob about his Sundays. "Do you ever go to church when you're on location?"

"Not as often as I would like. Since we work most weekends, I usually take some time and talk to God on my own and read some Scripture."

"Would you like to go to church with me?"

"I'd like that very much," Rob answered.

Abby beamed. Everything was falling into place for her.

Could life get any better?

"I'll race you to the old guardhouse," she said.

"You're on." Rob leaned low on his horse and yelled, "Ye-hah." Buttermilk charged after him, overtook him, and won the race by several yards.

"You've had a lot more practice," Rob defended his loss. "I've only ridden on location. You were born in the saddle."

"You're not too far off," Abby said and laughed. "Our whole family grew up riding morning, noon, and night. And I know this terrain like the back of my hand." She gazed fondly over the fort. "The new grass is doing well. The place doesn't look as if it were burned at all."

"The neighbor to the south let us cut sod from his land. We had to have matching vegetation or it would have looked fake. I meant to tell you that Emily asked Mr. Turner, but he absolutely refused."

Abby turned her horse and moseyed back toward the ranch. "I'm not surprised. He sure doesn't like this movie business. I'm glad you got your sod, but I thought you might use Astroturf," she said and laughed. "Everything is so fake about movies."

"We thought of it, but Astroturf was the wrong color. And it doesn't come in that tall a grass." Rob rode alongside Abby. "The neighbor was glad to sell his stand of pasture and let us replace it with better quality grass.

"Race your back to the ranch," he challenged and urged his horse into a gallop without waiting for Abby's reply.

On Friday night, Abby had Barb and Jack over for linguine with clam sauce, Rob's one specialty. Abby was relieved that there was no awkwardness between herself and Jack. In fact, he and Barb seemed to get along just great.

The difference between herself and Rob since their talk on the range was marvelous. Where before Abby thought they had gotten along wonderfully, now they seemed to float along with happiness dancing in their eyes.

When they all sat down for dinner, Abby reached for hands, as had been her custom since childhood. Rob asked the blessing, and conversation flowed nonstop.

"Jack, where were you in the shoot-out scene?" Barb asked.

"Over by the bank. My sister and her family were beside me. We ran out to the bad guy after Chase shot him."

"I was a saloon girl," Barb said.

"I know. I saw you," Jack admitted. "That was some dress you were wearing."

Barb actually blushed. Abby exchanged a look with Rob. Perhaps her little matchmaking scheme was going to work. Barb had met Jack only once before, when she had had another date and they had bumped into Jack and Abby at a restaurant. Now it looked as if something might develop between them.

After dinner, the foursome sat out on Abby's patio and talked, made sundaes, then talked some more. Around midnight, Jack told Barb he would follow her home to make sure she arrived all right.

"Did you hear that?" Abby asked Rob after the others had left.

"Could be something is developing."

"Wouldn't that be great? I think the world of Jack, and Barb is the best friend I've ever had."

"I'd like to replace Barb in that best friend category," Rob said and took her in his arms.

"Barb is the best woman friend I've ever had," Abby restated her previous observation.

"That's more like it," Rob said and kissed her, not once, but several times before telling her he had to go. "We're filming sunrise sequences tomorrow. But I'll see you tomorrow night. I find I can't get through the day without seeing you and holding you like this."

Abby had to agree.

thirteen

On Saturday morning Abby rose with the sun. The room she had worked so hard on all week was almost ready for furnishings. Before breakfast she had waxed the hardwood floor, and by ten o'clock, she had buffed it to a high shine. She spread her new oriental rug across the center of the room and stood back admiring the effect.

Getting the desk upstairs was next, and Abby knew it would be an engineering feat. She had asked her brothers over to help. Still feeling they owed her for getting them parts in the movie, they couldn't refuse her request.

Abby hung mini-blinds at the windows, then framed them with forest green drapes while she waited for her brothers to arrive. Ted came first, followed by her brother-in-law, Merle, who dragged Elaine with him. Her other brothers, Reece and Doug, arrived ten minutes later.

"Where are the doughnuts?" Reece asked. "You have to pay the workmen."

"After the desk is upstairs," Abby said.

Amid groans and grunts, the desk was carried step by step up the stairs and into her new study.

"What a room," Elaine said, once the desk was set in place. "What are you going to do up here? Surely not work for the tourist bureau?"

Abby hesitated, then took the plunge. "I thought I'd try

159

my hand at freelance writing. Maybe an occasional travel piece for a magazine."

"Wow," Reece said. "That's wonderful. You're a natural for it. You've written lots of stuff for the bureau. About time you wrote for yourself."

"You mean it?" Rob had given Abby the confidence to mention it to her family, and now they seemed sure that she could do it, too.

"You can do anything you put your mind to, little sister," Doug said. "You've shown us that over and over."

Abby couldn't believe what she was hearing. Mostly her brothers teased her. This type of encouragement wasn't their style.

"I'll bet Rob could give you some pointers," Reece said. "He seems like a nice guy. You ought to bring him over sometime."

"He's going to church with me tomorrow," Abby announced. "And he'll be at Mom's for Sunday dinner. So, please, everybody be on your best behavior."

"Does he like kids?" Ted asked. "It's usually a circus at Mom's."

"I don't know. We haven't discussed children."

"You haven't discussed children as in having some of your own?" Reece teased.

This was more like what she expected.

"We haven't discussed children at all. Now listen, guys. You leave Rob alone. Elaine and Merle have already given him the fifth degree. He passed, right?"

"Right," Elaine said.

"Besides," Abby added. "He won't be here long. He'll

be going back to California soon." Just when everything was going so well, she had to remember that the end was in sight. Would he write to her? Or would she be just one more in a long chain of on-location romances?

That wasn't fair. He'd given no reason for her to believe that what they had together was standard fare. Their relationship was something special. For both of them.

Please make it so, God, she prayed.

After her brothers had eaten all the doughnuts she had picked up earlier that morning, they left. Abby spent the next hour organizing office supplies in her desk and on the closet shelves and wishing the furniture store would deliver her bookcases. Not until after lunch did the delivery man ring the doorbell. He and Abby struggled to get the bookcases upstairs and set in place.

One upstairs bedroom served as Abby's storage room. From there she dragged some boxes of books and began unpacking. Unfortunately, dusting and sorting took a back seat to flipping through the books. When she pulled yearbooks out of a box, she settled back for a look at her past. That was where Rob found her at seven o'clock.

"I had no idea it was so late," she explained. "Just give me a few minutes and I'll be ready."

"That's okay. This room looks great. Do you have other books to unpack?"

Abby waved toward the spare bedroom. "About eight more boxes. But I can do that later."

"If you're not starved, we can work a while and have a late dinner. I know how exciting it can be to finish a project."

Rob carried box after heavy box of books into the study. Abby dusted them and arranged them on the shelves.

"I need a few knickknacks or pictures interspersed on these shelves. Break up the line of books."

"Have you read all these? *Organic Gardening*?" He held up one book.

"It was on the discard shelf at the library. I bought it for a quarter."

"You never know what you'll use for research, once you start writing your novel."

Abby smiled. "You're absolutely right. And I think this will be the week to start."

"Then we need to get that computer. How late are the stores open?"

"The one at the mall is open until ten. There was an ad in today's paper."

"Let's finish this up and check it out."

An hour later Abby was the proud owner of a computer. Her faith in Rob's knowledge of computers and prices let her make such a major purchase after checking only the previous week's ads for her comparison shopping.

"I never would have believed I'd have my own computer. It's different from the one at the office, but I'm sure I'll get the hang of it."

"The word processing program is the same as mine, so I can teach you its basics. In a couple of days you'll be a pro."

"I'm overwhelmed," she said, "and absolutely famished. Shall we rustle something up in the kitchen? The caramel popcorn we got at the mall isn't going to do it for me."

"I'd planned on taking you to The Steak Out. Sid's eaten out there and says the food is out of this world."

"I'll be ready in ten minutes," Abby said.

"Okay. I'll hook everything up while you change."

Within a half-hour, Abby and Rob entered the restaurant. Just finishing their meals across the room were Miss Penny Lynn and Sid. Sid waved them to his table. Miss Penny acknowledged their presence with only a slight nod of her head.

"Please join us for dinner," Sid said.

"Abby?" Rob raised his eyebrows in question.

"Whatever you wish," she replied.

Rob pulled out a chair for Abby, then took the seat beside her.

"I've been wanting to talk to you, Abby," Sid began. "I've not thanked you properly for all your help with the movie."

"You're welcome, but I've not done much. Besides, you paid me very well for my time." She thought of the computer that Sid's money had just bought her.

"I didn't mean the script. I meant help with the production part: getting the generator for us, putting us in touch with security, fighting the fire. How are your feet? Rob said you were fine now."

"Oh, that was just one night's annoyance. I couldn't be better."

"I find it interesting that you're always around when something goes wrong," Miss Penny inserted.

"Excuse me?" Abby said, wondering if she had correctly interpreted Penny's meaning.

"How did you happen to be at that fire? Aren't you the one who keeps seeing this phantom woman?"

Abby's mouth fell open and she closed it quickly. She would not dignify the actress's question with an answer.

"I believe I'll have the petite fillet mignon," she told Rob instead. "And a baked potato."

"Do you deny being the only one to see the ghost?" Miss Penny persisted.

"I've seen her, and she's not a ghost," Rob said. "She's as real as you are, Penny. We just don't know who she is or why she's sabotaging the movie."

The actress frowned, the line between her dark eyes destroying the beauty she obviously worked so hard at.

"Penny, I think you need a good night's sleep," the director said. "Sleep in tomorrow. It's a good thing we're taking the day off. I think everyone could use it. We'll get started bright and early on Monday, and if things go well, in another week or ten days you'll be off for your other project."

The waitress arrived and Rob gave their dinner orders. Miss Penny declined dessert, but Sid asked for cheese cake, prolonging the agony for Abby who was fervently wishing they would leave.

Rob asked the director several work-related questions and Sid asked about Abby's job, filling the need for conversation. Miss Penny remained quiet until Sid had finished his dessert and they were ready to leave.

"Will I see you later, Rob?" she said seductively. "I'll be up late."

Completely unruffled, Rob replied in an even voice, "I'll see you on the set Monday."

Miss Penny tossed her head and glided away without looking back.

"Don't pay any attention to her, Abby," Sid said as he took out his billfold and pulled out a credit card. "A woman scorned...." An impish smile lit up his face. "Dinner's on me."

"I'm sorry she acts like that," Rob said as soon as Sid had left them alone at the table. "She doesn't like losing."

"And she's lost?"

"Yes. Even though she wasn't in the race, she lost," he said enigmatically. "But I am sorry to put you through that."

"Don't worry. You'll be put through a lot worse tomorrow."

On Sunday as Rob sat beside her at church, Abby thought the minister could not have chosen a more appropriate subject for his sermon.

"We keep God out of a lot of areas of our lives. It's as if there are 'God: Do Not Enter' signs on newspapers, grocery stores, and car lots. We let God in when we discuss morality or at Bible studies or at a church service like today.

"Mark 12:30 reads, 'Love the Lord your God with all your heart and with all your soul and with all your mind and with all your strength.'

"Lots has been written about the Christian mind and how we should use it. A Christian mind based on what Jesus teaches and what the Scripture tells us becomes a framework for clear Christian thinking. No matter if the subject is political, personal, or historical, our thinking leads us to right Christian choices and behavior.

"As we go forth from this house of the Lord, let us carry with us the principles and beliefs of Jesus and apply them in our everyday lives."

Abby bowed her head. *I'm sorry, Lord, that I let the excitement of movie making and other distractions from routine take that Christian behavior away from me.*

Rob reached for her hand and squeezed it. It felt so right to be here in the familiar church pew with the man she loved.

Loved? Abby had to admit that she loved this man sitting beside her. But what could she do about it? *Turn it over to the Lord,* that voice within said.

Abby bowed her head again. *I love him, Lord. Please help me accept Your will where he is concerned.*

Rob drove Abby out to the ranch after the church service. They passed the fort, and Abby automatically looked for the mysterious old woman but saw not a soul among the ruins.

The Kane household was bursting with music and laughter and the high squeals of children's voices. Abby's older nieces and nephews had a radio on the front porch and were singing along with the top forty countdown. The younger kids were playing hide-and-go-seek in the yard, using the same old tree as base that Abby had used when she was a youngster.

"This is quite a crew," Rob said as they walked toward the front door.

"It does get a little loud."

"But fun," he added.

"Definitely fun," Abby said. Although Rob had met all of her family when the shoot-out was filmed, Abby refreshed his memory, not expecting him to remember the names of so many people. "There are twenty-one of us here today, counting you. And that's only my siblings and their families. When we add a few aunts and uncles and cousins, it gets positively wild."

"My sister and I seem quite subdued compared to this crowd," Rob said. "But I like it," he quickly assured her.

Before the buffet dinner, the Kanes stood around quietly while Mr. Kane asked the blessing.

"Thank you for our family gathered here today. Please be with each one of them as they go through the week and help them all to develop Christian minds. And thank You, Lord, for letting Rob join us today. Amen."

"Amen," Abby said quietly.

"I want the wish bone," one of her rambunctious nephews yelled.

"Me, too," another called.

"There are plenty," Abby's mother said. "I stuck them over here, boys."

Rob and Abby filled their plates and joined the grown-ups around the big dining room table. Instead of individual chairs, long benches sat on two sides of the table.

"We couldn't get chairs to fit and still have room for everyone, so Dad built these. He's quite a craftsman," Abby said, her voice full of pride.

"I hear you've been doing quite a bit of woodwork

yourself," her dad said. "Doug says you refinished a beautiful desk."

"A heavy, heavy, beautiful desk," Reece added his opinion.

"It took all four of us to get that upstairs," Ted inserted. "Where were you, Rob, when we needed you?"

"Sorry I missed that," Rob said and laughed. "But I got to carry eight boxes of books."

"Are you ready to start writing?" Elaine asked.

Rob glanced at Abby with a question in his eyes.

"I told them about my dream of freelancing. They think I can do it," she explained.

"Of course you can," her mother said. "You're one talented person."

"I bought a computer yesterday," Abby announced. "With Rob's help. It's different from the one at work, but Rob's going to teach me how to use the new word processing program."

"I'll give you the first lesson later this afternoon," Rob said.

"Uh-huh. Computer lessons. That's a good one," Reece teased. "Is that the new bachelor phrase? Instead of come up and see my etchings, now it's can I give you computer lessons?"

Abby glared at Reece. She had told him to be on good behavior and here he was teasing Rob.

"Whatever works," Rob said, and the entire family laughed.

"I recall that Reece gave Celia nightly guitar lessons, although he could barely finger the chords himself," Mrs.

Kane pointed out. "And Ted, what was your excuse to see Pam? Wasn't it to help her with a math class? And didn't she get a higher grade in the class than you did?"

Ted grunted. "Hey, Merle was worse than me. He gave Elaine riding lessons and she'd been riding horses since she was two years old."

"Yes, but he didn't know that," Elaine said with a smile.

"Do you already know how to use that word processing program?" Rob innocently asked Abby. The family burst into hysterics.

Abby really didn't know the program, but she learned fast. That Sunday afternoon Rob showed her the basic commands. After he left and throughout the next day, she read the book and practiced. By Friday afternoon, Abby sat in her study alone and caught herself smiling.

"Thank You, God, for this marvelous room," she said. The room was everything she wanted it to be. A telephone sat on the corner of her beautiful desk. Stacks of paper and envelopes lined the closet shelves, along with pens and computer disks. Her books were easily accessible now. And the plot she had been mulling over in her mind was taking shape on the computer screen.

Rob had convinced her to write the outline first, then to add to it as she needed. She thought he was right. It was a logical place to begin, and she was glad he was her teacher.

He was taking her to dinner that night and was to pick her up at seven, but at six he called.

"We're filming in the rain tonight."

"I didn't even know it was raining."

"It's not yet, but the weatherman promised us it would

be here within the hour. So we're headed out to Fort Phantom Hill to shoot. We need rain shots so the bandit can dig and find the treasure. Glad Mother Nature has finally cooperated with us."

"Have you already eaten? I could bring out tacos," Abby volunteered.

"That would be great. I doubt if I have any changes to make tonight, but Sid wants me out there anyway. I'll see you later. Oh, hot sauce, please."

"You got it," she said and smiled as she hung up the phone.

Abby hadn't been to Fort Phantom Hill since the Saturday after the fire. The filming had concentrated on Buffalo Gap, and she had been too busy to go watch it. Besides, she much preferred to watch the film crew work at the fort.

There had been no other sightings of the old woman, nor had there been any more acts of vandalism. Security guards patrolled the area night and day.

Abby stopped by a taco stand and picked up supper. It wasn't yet seven during the height of summer, but she turned on her head lights as she drove to the fort. Dark clouds skidded across the sky, blocking out the western sun. Big drops splattered on the windshield. This was definitely a Texas thunderstorm at its finest. Abby only hoped it wasn't accompanied by tornadoes that sometimes dropped from the clouds.

With an eye to the sky, she parked and awkwardly climbed out of the car, trying to raise an umbrella with the door opened only a crack. Getting the sacks of tacos and drinks out of the car was another feat of clumsy maneuvering. She locked the car and dashed to the trailer where Rob worked, finally reaching safety just before the storm unleashed its fury in the form of hail.

Inside, it sounded as if a giant were dumping a bucket of marbles on the metal roof. The trailer was crowded with raincoated technicians and crew members. Rob took the sacks and stowed them on a counter. "We'll get to that after the worst of this passes," he told Abby.

"I thought you wanted to film in the rain."

"Yes, but what is this nonsense?" Emily asked. "We don't even have thunder in California."

"Do you have a radio in here?" Abby asked. "We need to listen for threatening weather reports."

"I have news for you," Emily said. "We don't need a radio. I can tell you this is threatening weather."

"No, threatening weather is a tornado or a flash flood. Trust me, we need a radio."

"There's not one out here," Emily said.

Abby reached for the telephone and called her mother. "If we're in danger here, call us," she said and gave her the number.

It proved unnecessary, for the hail stopped after another ten minutes, although the rain continued.

Sid, covered from head to toe in rain gear, opened the door and poked his head inside. "Okay, back to work. We need the rain sequence."

The crew grumbled but went outside. When only Abby and Rob were left, Rob opened the taco sacks. "I'm starved. The chuck wagon served stew, but I passed."

"So the scene tonight is where the bandit digs and digs. Then Trice hears him and goes out. Right?" Abby asked as they sat at the table eating.

"Yeah. Penny has to get wet, too. She wanted that scene written out, but Sid said no. We got some great footage of the clouds rolling in. That's important stuff. Sets the tone of the scene. I'd like to watch the bandit find the money. Are you game?"

"Sure," Abby said and finished her last taco. "Is it now?"

Rob stuck his head outside. "Can't tell. Let's hustle over there. It's the climax of the movie."

He shrugged into a raincoat and helped Abby with an extra one. They shared Abby's umbrella and walked out in the semidarkness to watch the filming.

Not too exciting, Abby thought as they watched the man dig and dig beside the wall of the old commissary warehouse. She knew they would only use a few moments of it on screen, but the hole had to be dug and it was insurance to have every second of the digging on film. She shifted back and forth beside Rob. Her feet were getting wet and felt uncomfortable.

"Once he gets down so far, they'll stick the strong box in the hole and cover it up. Then he'll have to dig it out as if for the first time," Rob whispered in her ear.

A few minutes later, the shovel hit an object.

"Did we miss them planting the box?" Abby asked.

"No. He must have hit a rock."

The bandit kept digging and turned up some rotten wood. He dug farther down and the next shovel contained a longer piece of wood.

The bandit held his lantern over the hole and then jumped back, dropping the light in his haste.

"There's a body down there!" he shouted.

"Keep the film rolling on camera three," Sid ordered and ran toward the grave.

The bandit actor picked up the lantern and held it down in the hole for Sid to see.

"It's a body all right. Emily, call the sheriff!"

fourteen

"Stay back," Sid ordered as crew members rushed toward the open grave. "Bring that strong box. Let's finish this scene before the sheriff gets here," Sid said. "We've gone too far to quit now."

Abby watched in awe as the film crew backed away and resumed their positions. Two men carried a strong box to the hole.

"Should we put it on top of the bones, Sid?" one of them yelled.

"Can't hurt bones. Go ahead. Move it."

The strong box was lowered into the hole and some dirt thrown on top. Cameras rolled as the bandit dug lower in the hole, hit the solid lid, put down the shovel, and gingerly lifted the box out.

While the bandit opened the lid, the hero, Trice, sneaked up from behind and tackled him. By the time the ensuing fight was over, both men were covered with mud and Trice stood over the defeated outlaw. Penny had shown up holding a shotgun.

Trice then pulled the guy to his feet and at gunpoint forced him to carry the strong box to the stone building at the entrance to the fort.

"Cut. That's a print. That's all we need to get filmed in this rain," Sid said. He ran up to the grave and looked in.

Others followed him.

"Stay here," Rob told Abby and joined the others, then returned to her.

"Looks old to me, but I'm no forensic scientist. Was there a cemetery here? No, a body wouldn't be buried right next to the wall. Has there been any unsolved murder around here?"

"Not to my knowledge. Rob, this is gruesome." She watched as the county sheriff's car drove into the fort.

The sheriff and a deputy in transparent raincoats jumped out of the car. They strode to the grave and peered in, then got shovels out of the trunk of their squad car and enlarged the grave.

This time the digging did not seem boring as it had when the bandit was looking for the strong box. An ambulance drove up a few minutes later.

"I think a hearse would have been more appropriate," Abby said.

It was over an hour before the body was exhumed and en route to the Abilene crime lab where tests could be performed on the skeletal remains.

"What a night!" Abby said later as she pulled up in front of the hotel.

"Want to come in for a cup of coffee?" Rob asked.

Abby agreed, and they walked into the hotel coffee shop where others from the movie company had assembled.

"I think the old woman who set the fire was trying to keep us from finding the body," Abby overheard from the table next to them.

"Rob," she said and clutched his arm. "I think that man's

right. I'll bet the old woman was protecting the grave of her lost lover."

"What if the old woman killed her lover and buried him there? Now that would be motive for sabotaging the movie."

"We ought to call Ted," Abby said. "I know it's out of his jurisdiction, but he would want to know this kind of thing since he's been working security out there."

"Go ahead, I'll order."

Abby found the pay phone and called her brother. He joined them in the restaurant within ten minutes.

"I called the crime lab," he told them. "Unofficially they believe it's the body of a young woman and that the grave is over fifty years old. That's unofficial, you understand. They're running tests as we speak, but it may be a week or more before cause of death and other important information is known."

"A young woman!" Abby exclaimed. "To think I'd spent hours and hours at the fort and never known she rested there. Or didn't rest. But she can't be the woman we've been seeing."

"Of course not, Abby," Ted said. "There is no such thing as a ghost. A ghost didn't start that fire. A ghost doesn't carry a gasoline can."

"I know that. But I sure don't have an explanation for it," she said and took a sip of her coffee.

"I don't either. Maybe in daylight and without the rain, we can find some clue in the grave to indicate age or even a name. Sometimes murder victims are buried with identification."

"Doesn't it rot with the body?" Abby asked.

"Depending on what it is," Ted answered. "I think I'll go take a look at the site. I'll let you know if anything turns up," he said and left.

"I'd better go, too," Abby told Rob. They walked out to her car, sharing her umbrella. "Are you shooting at Fort Phantom Hill tomorrow?"

"We intended to, but if the sheriff ropes off the grave, we may not get to. I'll call you," he said and kissed her not once, but three times, before he dashed back through the rain to the hotel.

By Saturday morning the rain had stopped and the sun was as brilliant as ever. Abby woke up early and worked on the outline of her novel. Her mind kept going back to the grave of the unknown woman at the fort.

Since she couldn't concentrate on her writing, she decided Saturday morning was an excellent time to pay her mom and dad a visit. She wasn't fooling herself. She really wanted to go by the fort and see what was going on. If anything.

As Abby neared the fort, she noticed there were more cars than on that first Saturday morning shoot when she had met Rob. He had told her they had more spectators these days, since the extras felt it was their right to be on location in case someone was needed for a walk-on part.

Abby parked and weaved through the throng toward Rob's trailer. Ted was over by the grave, which was marked off with yellow tape that read "Police Line—Do Not Cross." She spotted Barb and two of her teacher friends. Then she saw Elaine and Pam and their kids, spoke to them for a moment, and learned that her mother had just left. Elaine reported that Rob had gone into his work trailer.

Abby had climbed the three steps to Rob's trailer when she happened to look back. From her higher vantage point, she saw old Mr. Turner walking across the field behind the fort toward the commissary warehouse. Something about him arrested her attention. He wore a baseball cap pulled low on his forehead, so that if she hadn't known it was him from his gait and the way he wore his clothes, she couldn't have identified him.

She jerked open the trailer door. "Rob, come look," she called inside without taking her eyes off old Mr. Turner.

Rob joined her. "Look," she said and pointed at her old neighbor.

"Isn't it Mr. Turner?" he asked, sounding mystified.

"Watch him."

"He walks like an old man."

"Or an old woman," she said triumphantly.

"You think Turner is the old woman?"

"It just struck me as I saw him. The walk is why we have always thought of the phantom woman as old. Let's go talk to him."

She pulled Rob along with her and cut through the throng of people to get to Mr. Turner.

"What exactly are you going to say to him? 'Have you been impersonating an old woman?'" Rob asked.

"Maybe."

Abby didn't have to say anything. As they approached Mr. Turner, he rounded the corner of the commissary warehouse and saw the police barricade. His hand flew to his mouth and he turned a ghostly white.

Abby and Rob hurried to his side.

"They found Martha," he said in such a low voice Abby had to strain to hear him.

Rob grabbed Mr. Turner to hold him upright, for the old man looked as if he would collapse.

"Martha, Martha," he whispered.

"Who's Martha?" Abby asked quietly.

"My Martha. My wife," he said in a quavery voice.

"I'll get Ted," Abby said to Rob and quickly ran to get her brother.

Both Ted and the other security guard returned with Abby. Rob had seated Mr. Turner on the ground. The old man had regained some of his color and more of his spirit.

"Are you the old woman who haunts this place?" Abby asked before Ted could take over.

"You saw her, didn't you? She scared you, didn't she?"

"You dressed in women's clothes. And you started the fire to stop the filming so Martha's body wouldn't be discovered. Why did you kill her?" Abby had no idea why she asked that last question. It just popped out.

"She was running away. With him. I couldn't let her go."

"Let's get him to a trailer," Ted said.

With Rob on one side of Mr. Turner and Ted supporting him on the other, they walked the old man to the trailer. The crowd seemed hushed, as if they knew what was going on. People moved apart to make way for the strange parade. In the trailer, Ted called the sheriff's office.

"Mr. Turner, you're under arrest for the murder of

Martha Turner. You have the right to remain silent." Ted continued to read Mr. Turner his Miranda rights.

When the sheriff arrived, he handcuffed Mr. Turner, again read him his rights, and escorted him to the patrol car. In a whirl of lights and the scream of the siren, the old man was taken away.

"I'll bet if we went to his house, we'd find the dark skirt and light blouse and bonnet," Abby said. "Can you imagine what he's gone through all these years? I'll admit he's always been odd, but disguising himself as a woman...." She shivered, and Rob put his arm around her shoulder.

"I believe I'll go see what I can find out," Ted said. "I'll let you know anything."

"Well, I was headed to Mom's when I dropped by here. I might as well go on over," Abby said.

"May I go with you?" Rob asked. "I'm due a break."

"Sure." Abby said, glad to have his company.

Around the Kanes' kitchen table, they drank coffee with Abby's parents and discussed Mr. Turner.

"He told me that his wife had liked glassware," Mrs. Kane said. "I thought it odd that he would continue the collection in such an obsessive way when rumor said that his wife had run off with another man. Maybe he was making atonement in some manner. He had room after room of the stuff."

"What will happen to his collection now? Does he have any relatives?" Abby asked.

"I don't think so," Mr. Kane said. "I believe he was all alone in this world. If you'll excuse me," he said, getting up from his chair. "I've got to check on Daisy. She'll have her calf today or tomorrow."

"Mind if I go with you?" Rob asked.

The two men left. Mrs. Kane poured another cup of coffee for herself and Abby.

"Rob's a fine Christian man," she said.

"Yes," Abby agreed.

"He's the one, isn't he?"

"The one?" Abby knew where her mother was headed with this, but she didn't know what to say.

"The one you've been searching for all these years."

"We're from different worlds."

"Nonsense. Same planet, same country," her mother said.

"But not the same state. I'm from Texas. I belong here. He's from California."

"Again, nonsense. I'm from Oklahoma. Do you think I said no to your father just because he wasn't from my home state?"

"Well, that's not really an issue. Rob hasn't asked."

"Abby, he'll ask. And when you marry, you go where work is and you make a home there. I'll admit, Texans are a special breed, but they can adapt."

They heard the men approaching the kitchen door and changed the subject.

"Daisy's fine. Not her time yet," Mr. Kane announced. He looked at Abby with a wistful smile.

"Well, Dad, it can't be long," Abby said, mystified by his tone. "Didn't you say maybe tomorrow?"

"Oh, sure. She'll do fine. She's never had trouble." He

kept his eyes on Abby, then glanced at his wife as if communicating a secret.

"Abby," Rob said, "I need to get back to the fort. Would you give me a ride?"

"Okay. Mom, are we on for dinner tomorrow? Did you ask the others?"

"They'll all be here," Mrs. Kane said.

"I'll bring dessert," Abby said. "See you then."

"Thanks for the coffee and the conversation," Rob said in a serious voice and shook hands with Mr. Kane.

Abby drove the short distance to the fort.

"Abby, would you come with me for a few minutes?" Rob asked.

"Of course. Do you need to talk about the script?"

"No. Not the script." He took her hand and led her across the road and field to Abby's prayer tree.

"Are you in a thinking mode?" he asked, once they sat down on the ground and leaned against the tree.

"A curious mode. What's wrong?"

"Nothing's wrong exactly. I'm going back to California on Tuesday."

Abby felt her heart fall to her toes.

"Tuesday? But they're not through filming," she protested.

"We don't lack much. Monday's shoot should do it for Penny. Chase doesn't care about rewrites. He says what's given to him. If Sid needs me, he'll call, and I'll fax him the changes."

"I see," Abby said carefully. She didn't want to cry, but felt tears welling beneath the surface.

"I'd like to come back," Rob said softly.

"You would?"

"Yes. If I bought some boots, do you think I'd pass for a Texan?"

Abby was afraid to believe that he would move to Abilene. She didn't trust her voice, so nodded in the affirmative.

"Would you share your new study with another writer?"

Again she nodded.

"And would you marry me?"

"Oh, Rob," she said and flung herself in his arms. "Of course, I'll marry you."

He kissed her, then Abby drew away.

"Rob, won't you miss the Hollywood life? You don't have to move here. I can leave Texas," she said. She'd never thought she could, but now she knew differently. Faced with the choice, she knew love was a much stronger emotion than loyalty to a place.

"Your job is here, your family is here, and you love it here. As long as I have a mailbox, a telephone, and a fax machine, I can be anywhere and write. There are times when I'll need to be in California, but there are airplanes from here."

"When will you come back?"

"I need to tie up some loose ends, give up my apartment, and ship some furniture back here. I'd say two or three weeks."

"Wonderful. We can tell my family tomorrow at Sunday dinner."

"I spoke to your dad already."

"When you went out to the barn?"

"Yes. He gives us his blessing, even though we've only known each other such a short time. He said he knew he wanted to marry your mom after two hours."

"My dad's always been a quick decision maker. That was thoughtful of you to talk to him. Very old-fashioned for a jet-setter."

"I wanted to do this thing right. When the spark's there, you just can't fight it."

Abby leaned over and kissed him.

"And the spark is most definitely there!"

epilogue

"That was the best movie I've ever seen," Barb said as she lifted her punch cup in a toast. "To the extras. And the writers."

The Kane family members and friends lifted their cups, much as they had five months earlier at Abby's wedding.

"My favorite part was the close-up of me walking out of the saloon," Barb continued. "And my second favorite part was when I ran out to Trice in the street."

"And your third favorite part was Trice taking your hand," Abby said and laughed.

The premiere had been a grand success. The after-party in the lobby had moved to Rob and Abby's house.

"It was all so realistic," Elaine said. "Especially the part in the rain when Trice fought the bandit."

"That part only reminded me of Mr. Turner, since that's when Martha's body was found," Abby said. "I feel so sorry for that man. To be in prison at his age, when he was actually in a prison of his own making most of his life."

"I'm going back tomorrow night to see the movie again," one of Abby's nephews said.

"I can't wait for it to come out on video," Ted said. "I'll be first in line to buy it."

Rob clinked a spoon against his punch cup, gaining the attention of the group.

"Abby and I have an announcement." He put an arm around his wife. "This is a special time in our lives. We're celebrating the movie that brought us together. And we've decided to collaborate on a project that's due next June."

"You're writing a movie script together?" Elaine asked.

"No," Abby said and laughed. "Well, we are going to write together, but this is a more personal project. We might even name him Trice."

A Letter To Our Readers

Dear Reader:

In order that we might better contribute to your reading
enjoyment, we would appreciate your taking a few minutes to respond to the following questions. When completed, please return to the following:

Karen Carroll, Editor
Heartsong Presents
P.O. Box 719
Uhrichsville, Ohio 44683

1. Did you enjoy reading *Under a Texas Sky*?
   ☐ Very much. I would like to see more books
     by this author!
   ☐ Moderately
     I would have enjoyed it more if _____

   _____

2. Are you a member of *Heartsong Presents*? Yes   No
   If no, where did you purchase this book? _____

   _____

3. What influenced your decision to purchase
   this book? (Circle those that apply.)

   Cover   Back cover copy

   Title   Friends

   Publicity   Other _____

4. On a scale from 1 (poor) to 10 (superior), please rate the following elements.

___Heroine   ___Plot

___Hero   ___Inspirational theme

___Setting   ___Secondary characters

5. What settings would you like to see covered in *Heartsong Presents* books?

_____

_____

6. What are some inspirational themes you would like to see treated in future books?_____

_____

_____

7. Would you be interested in reading other *Heartsong Presents* titles?   Yes   No

8. Please circle your age range:

   Under 18   18-24   25-34

   35-45   46-55   Over 55

9. How many hours per week do you read? _____

Name _____

Occupation _____

Address _____

City _____ State _____ Zip _____

HEARTS♥NG PRESENTS books are inspirational romances in contemporary and historical settings, designed to give you an enjoyable, spirit-lifting reading experience.

HEARTSONG PRESENTS TITLES AVAILABLE NOW:

add a little MYSTERY to your romance!

TWO GREAT INSPIRATIONAL ROMANCES
WITH JUST A TOUCH OF MYSTERY
BY MARLENE J. CHASE

_____*The Other Side of Silence*—Anna Durham finds a purpose for living in the eyes of a needy child and a reason to love in the eyes of a lonely physician...but first the silence of secrets must be broken. HP6 BHSB-07 $2.95.

_____*This Trembling Cup*— A respite on a plush Wisconsin resort may just be the thing for Angie Carlson's burn-out—or just the beginning of a devious plot unraveling and the promise of love. HP5 BHSB-05 $2.95.

Inspirational Romance at its Best from one of America's Favorite Authors!

FOUR HISTORICAL ROMANCES
BY COLLEEN L. REECE

___ *A Torch for Trinity*—When Trinity Mason sacrifices her teaching ambitions for a one-room school, her life—and Will Thatcher's—will never be the same. HP1 BHSB-01 $2.95

___*Candleshine*-A sequel to *A Torch for Trinity*—With the onslaught of World War II, Candleshine Thatcher dedicates her life to nursing, and then her heart to a brave Marine lieutenant. HP7 BHSB-06 $2.95

___*Wildflower Harvest*—Ivy Ann and Laurel were often mistaken for each other...was it too late to tell one man the truth? HP2 BHSB-02 $2.95

___ *Desert Rose*-A sequel to *Wildflower Harvest*—When Rose Birchfield falls in love with one of Michael's letters, and then with a cowboy named Mike, no one is more confused than Rose herself. HP8 BHSB-08 $2.95

LOVE A GREAT LOVE STORY?

Introducing Heartsong Presents —
Your Inspirational Book Club

Heartsong Presents Christian romance reader's service will provide you with four never before published romance titles every month! In fact, your books will be mailed to you at the same time advance copies are sent to book reviewers. You'll preview each of these new and unabridged books before they are released to the general public.

These books are filled with the kind of stories you have been longing for—stories of courtship, chivalry, honor, and virtue. Strong characters and riveting plot lines will make you want to read on and on. Romance is not dead, and each of these romantic tales will remind you that Christian faith is still the vital ingredient in an intimate relationship filled with true love and honest devotion.

Sign up today to receive your first set. Send no money now. We'll bill you only $9.97 post-paid with your shipment. Then every month you'll automatically receive the latest four "hot off the press" titles for the same low post-paid price of $9.97. That's a savings of 50% off the $4.95 cover price. When you consider the exaggerated shipping charges of other book clubs, your savings are even greater!

THERE IS NO RISK—you may cancel at any time without obligation. And if you aren't completely satisfied with any selection, return it for an immediate refund.

TO JOIN, just complete the coupon below, mail it today, and get ready for hours of wholesome entertainment.

Now you can curl up, relax, and enjoy some great reading full of the warmhearted spirit of romance.

— Curl up with Heartsong! —

YES! Sign me up for Heartsong!

NEW MEMBERSHIPS WILL BE SHIPPED IMMEDIATELY!
Send no money now. We'll bill you only $9.97 post-paid with your first shipment of four books. Or for faster action, call toll free 1-800-847-8270.

NAME _____

ADDRESS _____

CITY _____ STATE / ZIP _____

MAIL TO: HEARTSONG / P.O. Box 719 Uhrichsville, Ohio 44683
YES II